MANAGING AND OTHER LIES

BY
WILLOW HEATH

This book is a work of fiction.
Any resemblance to names and people, living or dead, is purely coincidental.
No part of this publication may be reproduced or transmitted in any form without written permission from the author.

Willow Heath asserts the moral right to be identified as the author of this work.

Cover design by Katarina Naskovski

Copyright © 2024 Willow Heath. All rights reserved.

For Issy
You keep me warm

TABLE OF CONTENTS

Managing 1

Chloe.Claire1 89

A Mother's Love 117

We Understand Each Other Perfectly 143

Baby 165

Little Blue Sticky Notes 185

About The Author 202

MANAGING

January 29th, 8pm

It's cold in here. Colder than I thought it would be.

When they sent me here, they told me to pack my essentials: soap, a week's worth of clothing (I would only find the time to wash them once a week, they said), and maybe a few books to relax with. The other things I needed, the house would provide. This journal was one of those things. They told me that writing in it would help. Help with what, I'm not sure yet. I'm also not sure if I'll keep writing in it. At least, not every day. But today is my first day so I'm making a few notes. And if it is going to help, as they say, then I should at least try.

They promised the job would be simple, and it looks as though it will be. Just look after the house. Keep it clean and tidy. Sort through anything that's a mess. Well, there is some mess but not an awful lot. And I'm not sure I'll always be able to judge what *is* mess. What if I throw out something that's important?

There's an office on the floor above this one (this one being the one I've set myself up in—there's a bed and a small window that looks out onto a path which snakes around the side of the house, and there's space for my clothes, and of course this desk for writing on). That upstairs office is full of cabinets, but the papers that must have belonged in them are now mostly strewn about the place: on the tabletops, piled up on chairs, even scattered across the floor. I don't know who did that or why, but sorting through that will be my first job. Or rather, I've made it my first job.

There's also a garden area around the back. A door in the kitchen leads out to it, as does the path I just mentioned. It's a simple square lawn with uneven, unkempt grass, a wooden fence covered with creeping vines (I think they're weeds), and a few flower beds around the edges of the lawn. They didn't say anything about weeding and keeping it tidy, but I think I'm going to. I like gardening. Or rather, I'd like to like it.

I tried to get a feel for the place before it got dark, but that proved to be difficult. The house is a bit of a maze. I'm not even entirely sure how many floors it has. I didn't get a good look from the outside so I'll have another wander around tomorrow. There's clearly a lot more that I haven't seen. A cellar and an attic, perhaps. There's a kitchen and at least one bathroom, and there must be a place to do laundry.

Once I've got a clear lay of the land, maybe I'll draw myself a diagram. And I'll make myself a calendar to keep track of the days. That's all for tomorrow, though. I'm tired now. I haven't eaten yet, but I'm not hungry. I'll get an early start tomorrow and sort myself out properly then.

January 30th, 6pm

This place truly is a maze.

I like the kitchen. It's warmer than this room. And I have just finished preparing myself a meal with what bits I could find leftover by whoever was here last (lots of sliced meats like packet ham and turkey, and plenty of milk that's still fresh). But the kitchen is quite far from my room. I considered moving myself closer to it but there's no other space on this floor that's ideal for sleeping. None that I could find, anyway.

Oh well, there's no harm in the walk, even if the days are currently too short and I have to fumble a little.

They said that I would have plenty of time to get the place in order, and enough to keep me busy. Occupied? Was that the word they used? Yes. They said that the house would be a distraction and a motivation. I'm sure that's what they said. Well, I'll be making a mess of my own as I go, and that'll need to be tidied as well. Like this plate beside me. I'll take it back to the kitchen and wash it up first thing in the morning.

I've had so little time to think about Catherine. My mind's on getting my bearings right now. I'm sure, as I settle into a routine and my thoughts have time to wander, they'll wander back to her. I assume she wouldn't mind, but perhaps she would. More for my sake than for hers, she'd say. Still, we have no control over the thoughts that creep up on us, do we? And when I think about her (which I'm sure I will), I'll do my best to focus on the happy things. The good things. She would approve of that, I know.

Perhaps it'll help to write them down here—those happy thoughts—when they come to me.

January 31st, 12pm

When they first approached me to take on this job, I thought it would be a good idea. I've spent so much of the past few years in motion with Catherine: travelling, working, getting tired, burning ourselves out.

This is good, simple, focussed work. Cleaning, tidying, organising. The kind of work that keeps the hands busy and the mind empty. Empty in a good sense. Pure and clean and calm.

Well, today I certainly did a lot of busying my hands and keeping my head empty. When I took my plate back to the kitchen, the morning light coming in over the garden revealed that the room was much dirtier than I initially thought when I first went over it yesterday. Plenty of dishes and cutlery to scrub. Stains on all the surfaces, on the wall behind the burners, that kind of thing. I got it all into a decent enough state today (which took a good while) before moving onto the other rooms. There isn't a huge selection of cleaning supplies. I'll have to go out and get more at some point. Most of the cleaning I did was with a fresh cloth and some warm, soapy water.

8pm

The day got away from me in the end, which I think is probably a good thing. I swept, washed, and cleared until the sun had set. I'm still not sure I've seen all of the rooms, but the ones I've gotten familiar with are now a little more under my control. I've tamed them; prettied them. I'm getting used to them, the way they feel, and I'm slowly getting them in order. Tidy, at least. Like I said, I need better supplies.

As I cleaned and cleared the various rooms, I occasionally thought about Catherine (like I knew I would). When I told her about this job, she said it would be a good idea, that it might be a healthy move for me. She's got her own life right now (a very good life that I'm happy about, happy for her) and I needed a good distraction of my own. She said that this kind of work, manual work, work with my hands, work on my feet, might help to calibrate my thoughts and my sense of self (to use her words). She wants me to be happy, I know that, and so I hope this job will be a step towards that. I'd like to show her a better, happier me, eventually. Not that I hope for anything. Like I said, she's happier now and a good person wants those they love to be happy. So now, I need to be happy too.

When Catherine and I first met, we were happy. But I lost my way and she had to spend a lot of her own time propping me up. Looking back, I see that clear as day. Now, she's looking to be happy again. She's focusing on herself, and she has encouraged me to do the same. We were happy for a while, but my thoughts got messy and I forgot myself. She has been so good to me for so long; she deserves to be happy on her own terms. I don't know how to do the same, but I've always listened to her advice.

She told me she met someone recently, but that she's not looking to them to make her happy. She just wants to find peace and joy and good things, and that maybe this person can be a part of that. I respect her outlook.

The house is cold and hollow, despite the clutter. I'm unusually conscious of the space and the emptiness, and of how alone I am. But being by myself—chewing on my own thoughts and getting in touch with my body and my actions—that's all good. I'm sure Catherine would think so.

February 1st, 5pm

Time disappeared again today and I forgot to make myself any lunch, so I'm having an early dinner now. That might mean

I'll be hungry later, but I'll just go to sleep early if that happens. An old trick, and one that tends to work.

When I was scrubbing the hallway floor today, I was very conscious of my breathing. It was loud. I don't think most people are aware of their breathing, unless perhaps they've been exercising. But there's so much quiet here. It was as though even my breathing had caused an echo, or as though it wasn't my breathing at all but someone else's. It was in my ear. Behind me. All around me. I wonder now if what I felt was a panic attack, brought on by nothing at all. Or by too much conscious thought going into my breathing. Maybe having an empty head isn't always a good thing. Now it seems I need thoughts to distract me from my breathing.

It's so quiet. Even now, as I write, I find that the scratching of my pen is deafening if I focus on it too much. The sound takes on a different quality, a different meaning. Like if you say your name too many times and it begins to sound alien.

Then I put my pen down and the silence floods in, like water into an empty container. But it's not water, not fluid, but more like ice. It's still and tense. If I focus on my head I get tinnitus. I get dizzy. Is it me doing that, or is it always there and I'm only noticing it now?

I'm thinking too much about these little tiny things; things that don't matter at all. If I focus on the abundant silence and the weight of every sound, I'll go mad. I can't write any more about this, but the act of writing does bring me a kind of comfort. I just need other things to write about.

February 2nd, 7pm

Today I went out into the garden. It's an overgrown plot of land at the back of the house, like I said, bordered by fences and those fences are being slowly, gently taken over by creeping things. At its longest bits, the grass comes up past my ankles and, upon closer inspection the flower beds are mostly filled with weeds. There are some small shrubs but the weeds are definitely taking over. I hope to work at it, to tame it a bit.

While I was out there, the silence remained but it didn't have that echo I could feel inside the house. The breeze and the openness carried all of that away. I paced around the garden and thought about what to do with it. What I would trim and cut and pull out. Maybe I could dig here and make some space and even plant something. Should I cut the vines down from the fences? Is there any point in doing that? I think maybe I should.

While I was asking myself these questions and trying to visualise what the garden might look like in the future, a man's voice cut through the silence behind me. Even as I write this, in the dim, yellow light of my room, the memory of that sudden voice gives me gooseflesh. It was deep, abrupt, like a thing let out of a cage.

He was standing and looking at me with his back to one of the fences. Perhaps he had climbed over, I wondered at the time, but that seemed silly. And surely I would've heard him do it. And who would do something like that? Maybe the fence has a gate in it that I didn't notice because of the vines and the creepers, but he knew it was there because, for whatever reason, he knows the house.

The man, with his arms folded over his protruding bowling-ball belly, asked me what I was doing. And so I told him with what I hoped was a polite smile. I'm deciding what to do with the garden, I said. He licked his lower lip and asked me what my plan was, exactly. I admitted that I wasn't sure yet, only that I wanted to clear out the weeds and tidy it all up a bit.

Tidy it up a bit? he repeated back to me, sounding like he was on the verge of being offended. How, exactly? I said that I wasn't sure yet.

He unfolded his arms, slipped them into his jeans pockets, and took a few steps towards me.

He was taller than me, and much broader. I felt as though his presence made me shrink, or maybe I really did attempt to fold into myself a little. He didn't get too close, though, and instead loomed over one of the flower beds and talked to me while looking at the weeds and jutting out his chin. He was pulling a curious face.

He told me what I should do. They weren't instructions, but they didn't feel like suggestions, either. I've now mulled over what he said then, and I do think that I should probably do as he suggested. That it would be the best thing to do for the garden. He told me what tools I would need and how long it should take, roughly, provided I do it all right. He seemed to know what he was talking about. I don't remember him leaving but he must have, through the gate that I didn't know was there. He didn't tell me his name or why he had come when he did, but I appreciated his advice and will do my best to follow it.

February 3rd, 10pm

I woke up to find that I had no milk for my morning coffee. No coffee, either. So I left the house and went to the local shop to get supplies, at last. Food, coffee, and plenty of better things to clean with.

This house sits at the edge of a small village. There are homes nearby but they are all clumped and gathered together—touching one another, or near enough. This house, however, stands alone, almost as though it is recoiling or keeping its distance from the others. It's large, with a puffed out chest and a cold demeanour.

The village itself is the kind that has more than likely been called *quaint* by every person who has ever passed through it without stopping. It has a local shop that sells newspapers and magazines, snacks and pet food, and a few of the essentials for making quick meals and cleaning the house. Everything I need, for now at least. The house is freezing at night and the heating system is so poorly designed. My room doesn't get enough heat, no matter what I do. And it only occurs to me now as I write this that there is no living room. None that I've yet found, anyway. No living room means no fireplace. I saw firelighters in the shop, and I can always buy a few newspapers and collect some wood, but there's no point if the house has no fireplace. Is there a chimney? I'll try and spot one next time I go outside, but the house is so tall.

I ended up buying only the simple essentials: bread, eggs, instant coffee, milk, and things like bleach and detergents for cleaning.

I'm sure there's more to the village that I didn't bother to see today. Surely there are scenic country walks around its edges (maybe some pockets of woodland and a little stream to follow). It would be nice if there was a cafe. Maybe there is. There must surely be a pub; every village like this one has a pub. It's probably a legal requirement of some sort.

When I got back and started to put things away in their proper place, I found a door near the kitchen that I hadn't noticed before; just beside the door that leads out to the garden. It's a kind of pantry, I suppose. I shelved a few things and then noticed a collection of wine bottles on the floor beneath the lowest shelf. I don't know who put them there and if I'm allowed to drink any, but I pulled one out regardless, found a glass, and started drinking. If the wine isn't for me and I've done something bad, I can always replace it. None of the bottles seemed particularly old or expensive.

I didn't get much work done after that, but I did see a woman.

She was standing in one of the doorways as I walked down the narrow hall on what I'm sure was the second floor. This hall, which I had not walked down before, was oddly thin and had several uniform doors lining either side of it. It must reach from one end of the house to the other to be so long.

The low evening sun coming in through the tall window ahead of me bathed the hall in so much light, I didn't see at first that one of the hallway doors was actually open. I only noticed her as I passed right by her, catching her silhouette in my periphery, which caused my heart to jump.

All I see now in my mind's eye, as I try to think back, is a woman's shape beneath a flowing dark dress, with ruffles and frill trim. It wasn't black, I don't think, but certainly dark. A deep red, perhaps, or purple. I don't remember seeing her face. The sharp light from the window must have obscured it completely, or I had simply drunk more than I'd realised and now my memory is hazy.

First a man and now a woman. Him, I understand. He must have wandered onto the property and wanted to give me some friendly advice. He might be a nosy neighbour who knows his way around a garden. Perhaps he's used to popping in. But she was in the house, standing in a doorway to a room I've not been in. And she said nothing at all. I hardly saw her (she probably thought I didn't see her at all) but she certainly must have seen me. She filled the doorway as I passed straight by. Does she live here, then? Was that her bedroom? Why did no one tell me about her?

It's late and dark and, even though I've been drinking plenty, I don't have the courage to go and find her room now, after sunset. The hall, the open door, the woman… I'm not ashamed to say that it all frightened me and left me feeling cold. But my curiosity is so lit up it has my skin itching.

If I can remember which hallway, which room, I'll go and knock on her door tomorrow. The idea that a woman has been living here since before I arrived, staying invisible and deathly still, has me shaken. So much stranger than this is why she didn't say anything when I passed right by her earlier, and why I haven't heard a peep from her since. Not a creak, not a footstep.

February 4th, 10am

I fell asleep last night while reading a short novel by a miserable author who died young, and in obscurity.

I woke up feeling particularly aroused and so I remained in bed, lounging and yawning and eventually masturbating to a fantasy about an old friend from university. A girl named Amy. In the fantasy, another friend (a boy named Jack) joined in.

The three of us were at a house party mixing cheap wine and warm cans of beer. Amy and I slipped away into an empty bedroom to play around. After a few minutes, Jack opened the door and found us there, but didn't laugh or call out. Instead, he shut the door behind him and joined in without a word. I lay on my back, submissive, and was fed her nipples and his dick one after the other, until she sat on my face and he gave me oral sex.

When I was done, I showered, applied moisturiser to the eczema on my hands (this always happens in winter), and then drank two cups of coffee to really wake me up.

4pm

Despite the low temperature, and the fact that I wanted to wait until it warmed up to do anything with the garden, I find myself unable to stop thinking about it. I want to be out there, getting grass stains on my knees and burying my hands in the cold, fresh soil so that they come up filthy and the dirt gets wedged under my fingernails.

Yesterday at the local shop, one of the supplies I picked up was a bottle of weed killer. I thought it wouldn't take much time or effort to apply it, even on a cold day when I don't want to be in the garden for long. So this afternoon, I went out and stood in the yard, investigating the state of the flower beds and the creepers on the fences. I half expected to see the man from the other day waiting there for me, eager to show me how to take care of the garden properly, but he wasn't there. The garden was entirely still in this February cold.

I took my time spraying some of the flower beds with weed killer, still waiting for him to suddenly appear behind me and offer some words of advice, but he didn't. I didn't stay out there long, but I doused every weed I could find in the stuff and hoped it would do something good, something productive, something useful.

8pm

The kitchen is never clean. I'm not much of a cook, and I'm not using that many things to prepare my meals with, but there is somehow always more washing-up to be done. More than the amount of pots and pans and plates that I'm using.

And it's not only washing-up to be done, but also stains to clean. Stains that I can't have made, but must have.

Perhaps I'm tracking mud in from the garden, even though the grass and soil is all so dry. Perhaps I'm creating oil stains on the wall tiles when I fry things, even though I'm careful to wipe everything down after I cook and before I eat. Perhaps I'm spilling coffee by overfilling my cup or stirring too vigorously with a spoon, even though this is nothing I've ever done in the past.

Before preparing today's dinner, I spent quite a bit of time scrubbing the various surfaces (the worktops and the wall tiles and the cupboard doors) and even the floor. When I was done cooking, I hurriedly but thoroughly cleaned up after myself before my meal had a chance to go cold, and ate it here in my room.

While I ate, I wondered if it's perhaps the woman I saw who's making the mess in the kitchen. Is she in there cooking and making a mess while I'm organising the house? While I step out into the garden to look it over? While I eat my own food in my room? I doubt it. I often pass the kitchen through the course of the day and never see or hear anyone in there. I never hear anything at all.

I'm sure I've already mentioned how quiet it is here. In fact, I've not heard the woman upstairs make a single noise whatsoever. Not a door closing or a creaking floorboard. This is the kind of house that wakes you up. A footstep here would echo there. Surely, even when I'm asleep, she isn't in the kitchen making food. I feel like, if she were, the house would let me know. So then, who is dirtying the kitchen? It must be me. And perhaps more importantly, when is the woman eating? And what is she eating?

Tomorrow, I must go and see her. Maybe she's sick and needs my help.

February 5th, 8pm

I don't know what I expected to find when I at last located the woman's room, except perhaps a sickly old lady in need of care (though I admit, that wasn't exactly the image I had in my mind, based on the fleeting silhouette I'd seen). I wasn't even sure where her room was, or even the location of that long corridor I had wandered down (I blamed my confusion on the fact that I had been drinking when I stumbled across it) but this is just a house, and so I assumed I'd have little trouble locating it.

And when I finally did find it, I would knock on the door, and what?

A few predictions came to mind: that she would be a frail, tender woman who needed looking after; that she was in fact the owner of the house and I simply wasn't informed about her for whatever odd reason; or perhaps that she was just a figment of my imagination. My wine-addled brain. That would explain why I never saw or heard her before or since that one fleeting moment in the hall. Had a trick of the light struck my drunk brain and convinced me that I'd seen a woman in a dark dress who didn't speak to or even acknowledge me?

I didn't find out which prediction, if any, was correct because I couldn't find the room at all. This has shaken me more than any revelation about her identity might have done. I was happy to admit that she had never been real at all, that I had invented her in a moment of stupor. But to invent an entire part of the house? No, that hadn't happened. Surely not.

This is, as I have said, only a house. A big, labyrinthine house but one that I have been living in now for long enough—a full week!—to know my way around. And yet I had managed to find that corridor only after drinking, despite having explored the second floor well enough in the days before. And I'm still confident there is a cellar and an attic that I also haven't yet found.

I put my pen down to rack my brain over why I walked down that hallway in the first place, the time that I saw the woman. Where was I going? Where had I come from? Where did I end up? My room, eventually, but before that? I couldn't have been on my way here because I come back here every day and never via that hallway. Not even always via the stairs.

I have just checked back through what I wrote on the day that I saw her. The second floor, that's all I wrote. And I had been drinking through the afternoon. I know the second floor well enough by now and I can't imagine how a hallway that I can no longer find would reach the entire breadth of the house.

It's all silly, isn't it? I had drank a bottle of wine to myself that day and yet I've spent several nights since thinking about the enigmatic other person that may or may not be in this house with me. Of course she was nothing more than a trick played by two pranksters: alcohol and a sharp winter's sunset.

The woman never existed at all. This is what I've decided.

February 6th, 6pm

I made myself an early dinner after working up an appetite. I sit here eating it now as I write, thinking about my thoughts.

When I first arrived at this house, I told myself (I may have even written it down here, now that I think about it) that I would focus on that office room filled with cabinets and papers. But exploring the house and daydreaming about gardening has since distracted me from that. And so, this morning, I entered that room and didn't leave it again until the papers were all in some kind of order.

As for what those papers were all about, there isn't anything of note, unfortunately. Nothing that I understand, at least. I'd hoped to learn something exciting about the house's owners or previous occupants. Something about their work, their family history, the house itself. A little gossip, to be frank. Something exciting.

Instead, sifting through it all left me with nothing but a headache. Thousands of sheets of paper, all covered with blocks of printed text. Thick text, printed with cheap ink. Diagrams and charts and tables filled with numbers. Documents and papers made up of jargon and digits and symbols.

I have no idea who the papers belong to or why they were kept in that room (and in that awful state, no less), but I couldn't make sense of any of it. Once I had decided that none of it interested or concerned me, I could get on with tidying and nothing else.

Nothing else except for the daydreams and musings that filled my head as my hands gradually sorted and filed by themselves. At first I thought about the woman who wasn't there and the man who was, but eventually (and unsurprisingly) my mind settled on Catherine.

I thought about her as I knelt down and shuffled the papers into folders; bound them with elastic bands and paperclips. I thought about her as I filed the folders away in the metal cabinets with no order or direction whatsoever.

Catherine and I had met in that singularly strange time between childhood and adulthood. That period of a few years where you're legally an adult (you have been for a while now, in fact) but you see nor feel no evidence of the fact. And yet you must take part in independent, adult life. As proof of us being children in adults' clothing, we met at a job interview and spent the day flirting back and forth. As it turned out, we were the same age. She had just completed a part-time postgraduate program at university, and I had been working my first real job—a job I deeply hated—for two years. During those two years, I had considered suicide more than once. I'm happy to confess that here.

(One day that I vividly remember even now: I was driving from my flat to my workplace, along a road which turned briefly into a bridge that passed over a busy road. A strong temptation took over me as I crossed that bridge, that I should turn the wheel sharply, crash through the barrier, and drop to my death. The only thing that stopped me, I'm sure, was the fear and the guilt of taking out a few other unsuspecting people driving below me; people who were also just on their way to work).

At the interview, a third person (whose name I don't recall) got the job. I do remember that they had interned there before, and so were pretty much guaranteed to get the job as a result. I also remember how terribly Catherine and I flirted through the day.

When Catherine and I left the building—herself feeling livid and me not feeling much at all—I asked her for her phone number. She moved in with me shortly after that.

As new adults with the carelessness of children, we decided to move abroad together. First, to the desert. Then, to an enormous and polluted city far away.

After making a habit of moving often, changing jobs and cities frequently, and avoiding the urge to let our roots grow, we eventually stopped seeing the world with wide eyes.

Some people get into a rut after marrying and having children. Others get into a rut by settling into a career much too young. We got into a rut by pretending our lives were hedonistic, when in reality our lives felt like a treadmill with pretty scenery passing us by like cardboard cutouts on a stage. But we continued to run on that treadmill for longer than we should have, and eventually came to hate each other for it. Catherine said she didn't want that for us, that we should separate for the good of ourselves and our relationship. If we separated, she argued, we could remain close enough, remain friends. Good friends. If we didn't, we may end up killing each other. Her words.

Catherine knows how to make herself happy. I don't. As soon as we separated, she made a beeline for happiness, and I came here.

February 7th, 1pm

The man was in the kitchen today. The man from the garden.

I woke up at around 9:30 and was in the kitchen by ten to make myself some coffee. And he was in there, washing mud off his hands in the sink. He had tracked in dirt on his boots and there was a crumb-covered plate next to the sink with a butter-stained knife resting against it. Was he the one causing the extra mess in the kitchen, I wondered.

I asked him what he was doing in here and he said he had been gardening. Well, not gardening so much as tidying up, he clarified. But, I protested, this is my garden to look after. He told me that I wasn't doing much of a job of it if that were the case. That I hadn't done anything at all since we last spoke. So, he said, I took it upon myself to help out a bit.

I told him I had sprayed weed killer on the flowerbeds but he didn't respond. He tipped a teaspoon of my instant coffee into a mug, poured in hot water from the kettle, and stirred. When he was done, he dropped the coffee-stained spoon on the worktop by the kettle and turned back to me.

I didn't do much, he said simply, just pulled out some weeds with a trowel and cleared some of the vines off the fences. Not much, but it's a start. More than you've done, eh?

I asked him why he was doing this and he simply said that he couldn't stand to see the garden in such a state anymore. That he was tired of waiting for me to pull my finger out and do something about it. That it would only get worse unless a man stepped in to take care of it. He said that last bit with a gritty, gravelly chuckle.

Anyway, he said after he gulped down the last of his coffee far too quickly, I've got a bit more to do before I'm done out there. Feel free to come give me a hand if you're free, he added, unless you don't want to get your hands dirty.

After he was gone and I was left alone in the kitchen (as I should have been when I first came in) looking at the mud on the floor and in the sink, and the dirty spoon on the worktop, I could only assume it was him that had been making the kitchen dirty after all. Does he live here, too, then? And if he does, why hasn't he properly introduced himself to me? And does this mean the woman I saw is real after all? If she is, she certainly needs my help, since she never makes a single sound.

I made myself some toast and tea and cleared up after him. I cleaned the sink and scrubbed the floor and returned to my room. I don't feel like doing much work today, and I certainly don't want to go out into the garden to help him. That was supposed to be my job. I was looking forward to it.

10pm

I've been drinking so this may be a little incoherent. But you'd be drinking too (whoever you are) if you'd had my afternoon.

After the man left the kitchen in a state and I cleaned it up (arsehole), I came back here to cool off but found that I couldn't. Eventually, I went back to the kitchen and peered out the window to see if the man was still in the garden. He wasn't.

He wasn't anywhere, as far as I could tell (so much for him putting in all that hard work he talked about) so I marched out there myself to do the work I had always meant to do—wanted to do—when the weather warmed up a bit or I found the time.

I picked up the necessary gardening tools and the bottle of weed killer and went to work. I grabbed fistfuls of vines with my bare hands and yanked at them, pulling them free from the fence boards they had latched themselves onto. I jabbed the trowel deep into the dry soil of the flower bed and brought up bunches of weeds, which I then tossed across the lawn. I sprayed weed killer into the cracks of the concrete slabs near the door like I was smoking them out or strangling them from underneath. I took a pair of gardening shears and snipped at the clumps of weeds that had gathered at the edges of the lawn, against the fences and the patio.

When I was finally satisfied with the work I had performed, I took a step back to admire how different it all looked. And it really did look different. The lawn was neater, the fences more bare and exposed. The flowerbeds could breathe again. It almost looked as though there was more room for sunlight to flood into the garden. It felt good, like some kind of triumph. My face and hair were soaked with sweat and my clothes were caked in patches of dried mud. It felt great to have made a change and have the marks to show for it. I did that. I could see it, and I could feel it. It hurt a bit and that was good.

I half expected the man to be standing nearby when I was done, nodding his approval or perhaps (and far more likely) telling me I missed a spot. But he wasn't.

The air was thick and cold and the sun was setting on an afternoon well spent.

I got back inside the house to warm myself up and purge myself of all that sweat and mud (I can't stomach the feeling of damp, sweat-sodden hair). I showered, threw my clothes onto the growing laundry pile, made myself some dinner, and found an unopened bottle of wine, with which I could rightly celebrate all my hard work.

As I returned to my room, the sun outside the window was low against the horizon, glowing a deep golden orange that lit up parts of the hallway and, by contrast, left the corners and doorways alone in darkness.

As I sipped at my glass of wine, I passed by an open door and once again caught a glimpse of the woman at the edge of my vision. This time, I stopped dead with purpose and turned on my heels. I wanted to see her, but of course she wasn't there. The doorway she had filled up, however, was now standing empty and led to a darkened room. I had drunk just enough, and felt bolstered by the last rays of sun on my back (as well as a fuck-you attitude towards that horrid man) and so I ventured inside the room.

It was a bedroom. Far more glamorous than the one I had chosen to occupy. The curtains (which were maroon and made from a thick, heavy fabric; tastefully decorated with a sort of filigree-like pattern) were completely closed across the large, high windows and there was a faint scent of fresh flowers. What flowers in particular, I couldn't tell you, and I also couldn't see any in the room.

The bed was a four poster; the posts themselves were a rich, dark brown colour and carved into spirals. On the lower half of the bed was a dark woollen blanket, neatly folded back over itself. It was the same red as what I had imagined the woman's dress to have been when I first caught sight of her.

On top of a chest of drawers was a decorative metal dish filled with tangled jewellery: necklaces, bracelets, rings. I rifled through it, (it being the only obvious thing to rifle through) and when I turned back to the bed, she was perched on the edge of it, looking at me with an unreadable expression.

She had certainly not been sitting there before, so I can only assume she had swept in silently when my back was turned. Had she intended to frighten me? Had she seen me nosing through her things? Of course she had. I didn't know what to say, and so I threw back the last mouthful of wine from my glass like it would give me some spell of courage.

The woman was middle-aged and wearing a white silk nightgown that reached almost to her ankles, with thin shoulder straps and some modest lace around the collar. *She looks vaguely like me*, I remember thinking at that moment; same nose, same brow, same hairline.

When I noticed my basket full of mounted laundry sitting on the floor next to her, I let out a choked chuckle (what an odd thing). She followed my eyes and looked down at the laundry, then lifted her frowning face and said that it wasn't good to leave laundry just lying around. I didn't know what to say in response (what would anyone say to that?) and so she filled the subsequent silence by asking me if I was cold in my room.

I told her that it was freezing when I had first arrived, but that I've grown used to it now. She said that acclimatising to the cold is not the same as being warm.

She then moved over to the chest of drawers (I had to side-step out of her way), bent down low, took a thick woollen jumper from the bottom drawer, held it out to me, and said that I could have it for a kiss.

One kiss, she said, and you can keep the jumper. It's a gift, really. The kiss is just a thank-you.

I accepted, and leaned in to give her a peck on the lips, but she hooked the long fingers of her hand around the back of my neck and pulled me in for a long and tender kiss. Her lips were warm and soft. She kissed me with a passion, and I felt my penis quickly stiffen under my jeans. When she was finally satisfied, she stood up straight and grinned before pressing the jumper into my hands. She shooed me away and simply said: Don't forget your glass as you go.

February 8th, 7am

I had a dream about Catherine. We were at an old country pub with exposed stonework and an open fireplace, sitting at an oversized wooden table: me, her, and someone she was kissing. Their arm was around her and she looked so happy. She was smiling and giggling as they kissed her, like she was being tickled. I'd never seen her so giddy. I was laughing, too, at the sight of it. I was having a good time. But my cheeks were damp with tears. We all ignored my crying like it wasn't happening at all.

10am

When I woke up, I half expected the woman to be in my room. My paranoid mind had not let me sleep for too long at a time. It kept waking me up to check that I was still alone. But why would she be in here, I asked myself. She has no reason to come in here. This is my room. *Perhaps I want her to come*, I wondered for a moment.

To relax before starting my day, I lay lazily in bed and thought about an old colleague I had once fancied. I masturbated to the fantasy of her and I having sex at work, at her desk, in the middle of the afternoon.

I'm at my desk, absorbed in my work, when she suddenly fills my doorway and announces with raised eyebrows and a grin that everyone else is out having lunch. She takes me by the wrist and pulls me over to her desk. She hikes up her skirt and takes off her underwear, and I slip inside her immediately, with no foreplay and no wasted words, knowing that we're on borrowed time and might get caught at any moment.

As I tugged on my penis, I felt another hand pull mine away, replace it, take a firm grip, and start to pull. My shoulders jolted and my eyes popped open as though I had just woken up, and found myself alone. Did I imagine that? Was it a dream or a fantasy?

Some days I hate having a penis. Others, I don't care one way or the other. I've always had it. I enjoy using it. Sometimes, when I'm particularly aroused, it even makes me feel strong. But that feeling comes infrequently, replaced instead with shame and awkwardness. Embarrassment.

Sometimes it's like it doesn't belong to me, or it shouldn't. Other times I tell myself that it's all right, that it's just an extra bit of me, but I often can't find the courage to say that and mean it. When I masturbate, the shame hides away. But when I'm showering or changing, and it's just hanging there like a dead thing, I hate it and want to be rid of it. And yet, I often think, it's funny that all my sexual fantasies involve me using it. Having it sucked on. Putting it inside someone else. More guilt floods in over that, but it's guilt that I don't really understand.

I hate my testicles far more, because they are where my shame is stored.

2pm

I'm out in the garden right now. It's a grim day and the air is sharp and biting. I feel comforted by having this journal with me to write in. I don't mind what I put down: thoughts, memories, ideas. It helps me to feel less alone.

When I came out here, I was disappointed by how little work I had accomplished yesterday. (Or was it the day before? For some reason, it's hard to recall.) I thought I had killed so many weeds, torn down so many vines. I know I had, in fact. I felt as though I had managed to let the garden breathe, given it some space and some light. I remember writing words like those in here. But now, looking at it all as I write, there are still so many things clogging up the flowerbeds and creeping up the fences. Ugly, obnoxious things. The edges of the lawn need trimming again. They're dishevelled and ragged.

Did the weeds come back or did I just not do as good a job as I'd thought? Surely the latter, which frustrates me. I worked so hard.

4pm

A fog has crept in over the past few hours, growing thicker and thicker, blotting out the sun and turning the world sad and grey. It makes the new progress I've made hard to judge. But I know how much space I've made this time. I'm sure of it.

The plants in the flower bed have room to spread their branches and grow new leaves when the spring comes. I know that. I pulled the weeds up, roots and all. I'm writing it down here as proof.

The fog is grey and wet, drifting through the garden like a heavy ghost. It's making the grass damp and so I won't be able to cut it today. But that's all right. I don't have to do it all today, or there will be no work left for tomorrow or the next day or the next day or the next day.

7pm

I came to the office full of cabinets. I wanted to read over some of the papers again, to see if I could decipher them, but they don't mean a thing to me.

It's strange, reading something that might as well be in a language I don't know. Even the titles, oversized and underlined, make no sense to me. Graphs that have one measurement on X and another on Y but show me nothing of value.

There's something frightening, almost dehumanising, about not being able to make heads or tails of what's written here. These are the only records in the house, and there are thousands of them. But records of what, exactly? All of it is meaningless to me. I hate that.

February 9th, 12pm

When I came into the kitchen this morning to make toast and coffee, the man was standing there, leaning his flat arse against the edge of the worktop, one hand across his saggy chest and the other holding a brown-stained mug of something to his lips. (Were those stains coffee or dirt?) His boots were filthy, and so was the floor as a result; he had been in the garden again. *My garden*, I thought.

When he saw me, he raised his eyebrows over the mug, took a loud sip, and smacked his lips as he lowered the mug.

You still haven't done much with that garden, he said. I insisted that I had. Twice, in fact. That I had used weed killer and pulled the weeds up by their roots and made space for the shrubs to grow and cut down the vines from the fences. He said that it looked like I'd hardly done anything at all. He puffed out his cheeks and said he'd happily do it for me if I couldn't manage it or I couldn't be bothered to do it.

I told him that I liked doing it, that I wanted to do it, that I *was* doing it, that it was *my* project. He didn't respond. He just smirked and snorted and took another loud sip.

He made me nervous standing there. He took up so much of the kitchen. It was impossible for me to move from the doorway and do anything until whenever he would finally decide to leave.

I breathed deep and asked him what he was doing here, in this house. Just taking care of what you're not bothering to do, he said. He put down the mug with a purposeful thud and shifted his weight over to the other door. Right, he said, better get back out there and finish up, since you're clearly not going to do it.

Talking to his back, I said for him to leave it alone, that I was looking forward to working in the garden today. Well, he said, you'd best crack on. It's nearly noon. I could've finished it by now.

Haven't you already been out there? I asked. He said no, that he was just checking on what I had done. Or hadn't. He snorted again. I asked him to please stop tracking dirt into the kitchen because I keep having to clean up after him. He laughed and said that I wasn't doing much else around here, that it wouldn't hurt to get my hands dirty and get some cleaning done. Then he kicked at his heels and let more thick flakes of dried mud fall to the floor like dandruff. He smiled and walked out, leaving the door open and the cold blowing in.

5pm

I don't know where the man went after he left the kitchen. I didn't see him again.

When I went out into the garden, it looked like progress had been made in clearing away the weeds and vines, but not enough. And now I'm not sure if it was me or him that got it to the slightly better state it's in now.

I paced around the garden taking deep breaths, trying to loosen up my stiffened shoulders and calm my twitching hands. The man had sent me into an anxious spiral and my thoughts were racing. I must have dug a groove into the lawn with the number of laps I walked.

Once again, I gripped at the vines with my bare hands and yanked with all my strength. They held on tight to the fence and it was satisfying to win the fight and prise them away eventually. I threw them into a plastic bin and didn't stop until the bin was full. Then I knelt down at the edge of a flower bed and tugged out handfuls of weeds, shoving them into the bin and forcing it all down with my bodyweight until nothing else would fit. When I was done, I dumped the bin in a corner of the garden and went back inside, huffing and panting and feeling a little bit better.

When I came back into the kitchen, I made coffee and scrubbed the dirt off the floor while the kettle boiled. I had to get down on my hands and knees to do it properly.

11pm

I ate my dinner in the kitchen. I had a glass of wine as I prepared it, and another with my food. I went back to my room via the hallway with the woman's bedroom, but her door was closed when I passed by.

When I was almost at the end of the hall, I heard her voice call out from behind me. She asked if I had been wearing the jumper she gave me. I said that I had, that it was very comfortable (and that was true). She told me she had more clothes I could wear if I wanted to come and take a look. I shrugged and followed her into her room.

More wine tonight? she asked with a raised brow. I nodded and she said that I should watch how much I'm drinking. I told her I would, and so she went to her closet to show me some things I might like.

We stood there together and I noticed then that she and I were around the same height and almost the same build. I've always loved how slight I am. I have narrow shoulders and all my fat goes to my hips and thighs if I gain weight. I felt like her equal as we stood there in front of a rail of hanging clothes, our shoulders touching.

She told me to pick out anything I liked, anything that might suit me. I filed through a few things, sliding them across the rail as I went, and stopped on a blouse that caught my eye. It was just my size; pitch black, with a high collar, small felt-covered buttons, long loose sleeves, and tight cuffs. I was about to take it off its hanger when she stopped me by gripping my wrist quickly and tightly. That's a woman's blouse, she said in a flat voice.

But you said I could pick anything out, I protested, and this would definitely fit me.

That's a woman's blouse, she repeated, her voice soft but firm. But why is that a problem? I asked. Her brow furrowed and her eyes shrank under its weight. It's not for you, she said.

I continued to search through her clothes and she watched me patiently (I had now become so tense and frustrated and irritated), but so much of what she had was what you might describe as women's clothing: dresses, blouses, skirts. I turned to look at her, wondering if this was some sort of game we were playing. She was wearing a shapeless nightgown and her salt-and-pepper hair was tied up in a tidy bun. Her face was unreadable, so I kept dragging items back and forth across the rail until I stopped at a denim jacket. It looked a little big and baggy for either me or her, so I took it and tried it on. It fit me poorly; loose in all the wrong places.

Well, she said, doesn't that look good on you. She placed a warm hand against my cheek and smiled. So handsome, she said softly. I smiled back, unsure how well I was hiding my discomfort.

For that one, I'm going to need something more than a kiss, she said.

Just like last time, she hooked her hand around the back of my head and pulled me in. Her fingernails—sharpened to a point—sank into the nape of my neck. Not enough to break the skin but sure enough to make me alert.

She pressed her lips against mine with more force this time, and thrust her tongue in-between my teeth without any teasing or softening of my defences. It tasted sweet. I eventually began to loosen up, getting lost in the sensation, when suddenly she bit down on my tongue. My eyes popped open and when I tried to pull away she only clamped down harder, drawing blood from the soft flesh of my tongue.

As soon as she tasted my blood, she started to trace her tongue around mine. She bit down again on the same spot and more blood leaked out. I could feel it, taste it; it made me queasy. I whimpered at the sharp pain of it. She licked at my teeth and the roof of my mouth, collecting my blood with her tongue. At last, she retracted it and then began to suck on my tongue, groaning at the taste of my blood. Her hands held my head firm and I couldn't move, despite trying more than once. One more time she sank her teeth into my sore, throbbing tongue and sucked more blood from it.

When at last she let me go, I stumbled backwards and placed a finger in my mouth. So much fresh, crimson blood came away on the tip of it. It felt as though my mouth was full of it, and my tongue was swelling.

She was smiling like a child. She licked her lips slowly, with a tongue covered in my blood, and said thank you. I asked her, with tears in my eyes, why she did that. I told her how much it hurt. She snorted and told me to be a man, to enjoy it, to live a little and be daring. Then, just like last time, she shooed me out the door. I went back to my room and wept until the bleeding in my mouth finally stopped.

February 10th, 8pm

When I first woke up, I didn't open my eyes. The raw throbbing pain in my mouth caused me to squeeze them tightly shut instead. I felt sad. Abused. Guilty, like I'd done something wrong. Like I'd done it to myself, that thing the woman did to me. Or like I had deserved it for some reason.

She had taken something from me and I hadn't wanted her to. I shed a tear at the memory of it, and then another for my shame. Then I swallowed all of that and opened my eyes.

On most days I wake up long after the sun has risen. I'm not what you'd call a morning person. And while today was no different, the lack of daylight which usually illuminates the closed curtains made me think the sun hadn't yet risen. When I at last noticed the wind and the rain rattling the windows, I felt something I've felt a thousand times: disappointment that I might not see the sun today, and a relief that today can be a pressureless day of rest.

That is to say, I decided that today was a day to clean the bathroom and do some laundry.

I'm not sure I've mentioned the state of the house's bathroom. The design is decades old, with beige tiles covering the lower half of every wall. A grubby, formerly white rug sits useless in the centre of a linoleum floor, its edges frayed and its colour now indescribable. The linoleum itself doesn't properly fit the floor; there are gaps where it doesn't quite reach one wall, and warped patches where it wasn't cut to fit the other wall. The toilet and sink match the tiles (a hideously creamy beige colour that leaves me feeling somehow sick), and I have so far only used the bathtub to shower because the room doesn't offer the kind of relaxing atmosphere needed for a bath. Though a long bath is certainly something I could do with right now. Maybe tomorrow I'll go out and buy some candles, turn off the bathroom light, and try to forget where I am.

When I arrived here, the bathroom wasn't sparkling new but it wasn't dirty either. Just old and unloved. This means that the only grime to clean was what I had made: mostly soap stains and water marks.

I put the bathroom back into a good enough shape, ready for me to hopefully have that bath tomorrow, and then went in search of the laundry room, which I still hadn't found. The situation was becoming desperate as I was quickly running out of clean clothes.

As it turns out, the laundry room is in the basement, the door to which is near the kitchen. It struck me as impossible, when I located it, that I had simply ignored it all this time. I'm sure I've mentioned here how I had a gut feeling that this house would have a basement, and it does; the door to which was hidden in plain sight, as it turns out.

The room beneath the house is freezing, with bare brick walls and a concrete floor. A single lampless hook light hangs from the ceiling in the centre of the room, casting deep shadows in every corner. It's a frightening room. In fact, if it weren't so convincingly frightening I would almost find its attempts to be scary kind of funny. It feels funny-by-design, but is in reality simply uncared for and used only for its barest necessities. Still, it has what I need to keep my clothes and towels clean, and that's all I need it to do, which was clearly also the attitude of the people who dumped the washing machine down here and did nothing else to make the room pleasant at all to be in.

After filling it up with dirty clothes, I left the washing machine running while I went back upstairs to potter about. But the thing rattled and shook dreadfully, and I could hear it from every room on the ground floor. No matter where I went, it echoed in the rooms and its vibrations passed through the walls.

When I went back down to gather my washed things, I wore the jumper the woman had given me, to protect me against the hard cold of the room.

With a bundle of wet clothes in my arms, I looked around for somewhere to hang them and found two large wooden clothes horses in the corner. They had several of my items already draped over them, which sent a shiver through me until I remembered how the woman had taken my laundry basket from me the first time we met. The strangeness and the stress of the last few days must have led me to forget that odd encounter almost completely.

When I went over to check on them, they were still wet and smelled faintly of mould. Nothing had any hope of drying in such a cold, airless basement. I took the still-wet clothes from the clothes horses and threw them back into the washing machine, then tossed my freshly-washed clothes in the basket. After the second load was done, I would take both loads upstairs and find somewhere warm and airy to hang them up.

The rain hadn't stopped all day, so I couldn't hang my clothes outside (not that the garden had a washing line anyway). The afternoon was just as dark as the morning had been, and when it was time for the sun to set, nothing much changed. A day had gone by with no sun at all, but the low, heavy weather had provided a strange kind of comfort. It felt as though the rain was a shawl, or like something that was alive, something to keep me company here. More comfort and company than these two people I had found and desperately wished would go away as quickly as they had appeared.

When I heard the washing machine stop, I went back down to the basement to collect everything together and bring it upstairs. I gathered all my wet, clean-smelling clothes into the basket and made for the stairs. In the deep shadows beyond the reach of the hook light, standing halfway up the stairs, was the woman.

She asked me what I was doing down here, but she didn't move. Her voice was calm but hard. Assertive. She had her hands clasped together in front of her, in a pose that was neither warm nor cold. I couldn't see her face at all. Her position, almost hovering above me in shadow, made me feel smaller in that moment than I ever remember feeling. I told her that it was a rainy day and so I was doing my laundry.

I was doing that for you, she said, you know that. Yes, I said, but I had more to do and now it's done and I'm taking it somewhere warmer to dry. But why did you move the washing I had already done? she asked. I explained to her that it was going mouldy because the basement is too cold and damp for it to dry properly.

When she moved to the bottom of the stairs, one heavy step at a time, I could see the state of her face. Dark and streaky makeup smudges—like she had been crying for hours. Locks of hair escaping in all directions from a poorly-tied bun. Her mouth hung open in a low scowl and I could see every one of her teeth. She didn't blink.

She moved towards me and I stood rooted to the spot, my bare feet freezing on the concrete floor. When she reached me, she grabbed the basket with both hands and wrestled it from my grip. I held it firm for one defiant moment, but gave in quickly enough (I couldn't bear to look her in her bloodshot eyes).

You ungrateful creature, she spat as the basket of wet clothes toppled to the floor. If you didn't want me doing your laundry, you could have just said something. And if my standards aren't good enough for you, you can do your own washing from now on.

When I replied, in a barely audible mumble, that that was exactly what I wanted, she slapped me across the face with enough speed and force that it caused me to stumble backwards a little. She had moved so quickly, with such confidence, that I had never seen it coming. The emotional shock of the slap hurt as much as its physical impact.

Without another word, she turned and marched up the stairs, and was suddenly gone. I heard no footsteps echo through the house.

February 11th, 11pm

I had to get out of the house today.

I woke up early, shower-shave-moisturise-makeup-coffee, and left the house as quickly as possible. The need for bath candles and a few other things was my excuse for spending the day anywhere else.

While I'd been outside the house once already, that was just a quick visit to the local shop. Today, I wanted to take my time and get to know the village that this house perches awkwardly at the edge of. It's a charming place; almost every building stands on its own and is made of brick or stone. There's the shop, but also a pub and a cafe and a pharmacy, just as I hoped there would be.

After buying a few cheap, unscented candles from the shop (it was all they had), and a few more things to cook and clean with, I decided to have lunch at the local cafe. It had an awning and painted white walls and a few unoccupied tables perched on the pavement outside. My plan was to tuck myself into a quiet corner, to enjoy a sandwich and a latte, and to read a book for as long as possible. Hours, if I could manage it (my anxious brain and racing thoughts might not let me, I feared).

The cafe's interior, as it turned out, wasn't big enough to have quiet corners. It was a small but bright and airy space, with just a handful of little wooden tables and a glass counter displaying fresh cakes and pastries. I did get my sandwich and my latte, though, and was eyeing up a slice of cake to enjoy a little later.

When I got up to order what I wanted, the woman beamed a warm and welcoming smile at me and asked, in the lovely local twang, if I was just visiting the village. I told her I was looking after the big house just down the road, and I vaguely pointed in its direction. She frowned for a moment, then offered me a pinched, apologetic smile, and said she was afraid that she didn't know it.

It was my voice that did it. It's always my voice. She saw me one way at first, as I tottered over to the counter, but then she heard my voice, and suddenly she saw me entirely differently. She was polite, of course (most people are), but I've seen that awkward shift in expression enough times by now. They see you as someone odd. Not bad, necessarily, but strange and difficult to understand. Unknowable. Imprecise, almost.

I often think of the famous people who get away with living how I do and are celebrated for it. But those people are entertainers; performers; clowns. They're here to amuse us. They're seen through different eyes, but not necessarily kinder or more accepting ones.

The point is: I can't mask or alter my voice. I don't know how. Part of me thinks I shouldn't have to, but that part often gets squashed down by shame and other bad feelings.

Still, the young woman served me what I ordered and I spent a good hour or two reading. I even went back up to order that slice of cake I had been eyeing up.

At one point, an elderly man brought me out of my quiet time to ask me what I was reading. I told him that the author was a Bohemian writer who died young, sad, and irrelevant. The old man looked me in the eye as I spoke, blinked once and with purpose, and then nodded to himself before returning to his newspaper.

Before coming to the house, reading alone in a cafe had been one of my life's simplest but greatest joys. I looked forward to doing it on weekends. Ordinarily, I can lose a whole day to it. But after two hours today I was done. This was partly because of the awkwardly intimate size of the place and the fact that the local people didn't know how to treat me, seeing me instead as a foreign body (and an impossible, irreconcilable mix of one thing and the other), but also because, while I had purposefully fled the house for the day, my mind was still very much trapped in there, nervous and afraid.

Still, I wondered how else I could put off my return. I couldn't stay in the cafe any longer, but I wouldn't go back to the house; not yet. This led me, as a temporary solution, on a long and aimless walk around the village and the nearby public footpaths across fields and through a small thicket of woodland.

It all looked like every other quiet, green part of the country, but that didn't mean it was any less pleasant. I once read that the sound of birdsong triggers the release of as many happy chemicals as a kiss or a piece of chocolate. Maybe more. It was healing, from the inside out. And I needed healing, inside and out.

The natural landscape (a hill, a stream, a small stretch of forest) dictated the path, rather than the other way around. This meant that the path had to contort itself into all sorts of ridiculous shapes in order to work as a path at all. Following it was fun. It kept my brain engaged and focussed on one thing only: walking that twisted, knotted line.

There was so much quiet there, but the quiet was also punctuated and disrupted by, as I said, birdsong. And the sound of trees rustling, flowing water, fallen leaves tumbling, wind blowing, dirt kicking up. These sounds were rich and colourful and calming. I felt connected to the world again, just for a short time.

Another solution to avoiding the house—after I was done with my country walk—was an early dinner and a few drinks at the local pub (as many drinks as were needed).

The Red Lion was made from stone, and its interior was so rustic that it had a low ceiling supported by warped wooden beams, and even a lit fire in an open fireplace which, given that it's still winter, was a welcome sight (and sound). I chose a small table near the fire, hung my coat on the back of the chair, and went to order a glass of wine. The woman at the bar was younger than me, and she treated me kindly as I ordered and paid for my drink. I took a menu back to my table to mull over while the sun slowly set.

Pubs have never been a place I've enjoyed. Call it prejudice or my own bias but I have always seen them as places charged with too much masculine energy. Rowdy men making grunts and noises that unsettle and intimidate me. I hoped that, on a weekday, around dinner time, this country pub wouldn't get like that. Catherine has always been the same. Over our years together, she and I spent half our free time eating, drinking, and reading at cafes and restaurants; never pubs.

Finding our favourite local coffee shop was at the top of our to-do list every time we moved to a new place. Aside from a glass of wine at home, neither of us have ever been enthusiastic drinkers, and so pubs had never managed to fit neatly into our lives unless we were dragged to one by friends. Coffee out, wine at home, that was always how it went. And while I have been rediscovering and reinventing myself lately—getting close to knowing and understanding myself—becoming a pub person is still not on the cards for me. My small feelings aside, if I could while away a few hours with food and wine and an open fire, I'd be happy. This didn't happen, though.

The same woman brought my dinner and a second glass of wine. As I tucked into my meal, I caught—out of the corner of my eye, across the room and in the other corner—what I was sure in an instant was the man who kept visiting the house. He was sitting alone, just like myself, but when I looked over properly, that table was unoccupied. I shuddered, but carried on enjoying my food.

Catherine is a vegetarian, and I had always been happy to eat the same meals as her because I know it's good for my health, but since coming to this place, I've occasionally cooked and enjoyed meals with fish and pork. Tonight I ordered the gammon and chips. The saltiness and thickness of the gammon left me feeling satisfied.

I finished my meal and my second glass of wine, then returned to my book. Like the elderly man in the cafe earlier, the woman from the bar came over to ask me what my book was about. I tried to sum it up and she then took a seat across from me and asked if I was new to the village. I explained my situation and, while she didn't seem to know the house, she explained that she had always lived here but she was hoping to move away soon.

I told her I had lived all over and that moving around is great. I certainly recommend it, especially while you're young and full of energy. That unshackled feeling is liberating.

When she asked if I was staying here by myself, I saw a flicker at the edge of my vision. I felt, at that moment, like I was being watched. Like I should choose my words carefully. If I had looked over to the other corner at that moment, I wonder, would I have seen the man? I didn't look. I kept my eyes locked on her and answered her questions. While she apologised for asking so many of them, I smiled, shook my head, and said that it was lovely to have someone to talk to, that I was going half mad looking after that house all by myself.

We talked for a little longer. She was kind, genuine, and interested in the answers I gave her. But eventually, she had to go serve a group of young men that had come in and crowded around the bar, so I carried on with my book alone.

I huddled into myself and held the book a little higher, hoping to avoid their attention. It wasn't something I needed tonight. Or any night.

Another flicker caught in my vision and this time I did look over, almost without thinking (the same way you think you see a spider or something else out of the corner of your eye when you're at home alone). The man was there, drinking a pint of something by himself. He looked at me, smiled with half his mouth, and lifted the glass in a lazy toast.

I turned away and back to the page. Part of me wondered if now was the right time to ask the woman serving at the bar if she knew the man sitting across the room, but she was busy with other customers and, besides that, I had an unsettling feeling that if I did ask her, she would only tell me there was nobody sitting there at all.

The very idea of it sent another shiver through me and I was now far too paralyzed to look over again. I read the same two pages three times, taking none of it in, and eventually turned the page.

A few chapters from the end of my book, I decided on one more drink. The young woman was busying herself when I went over and asked for another glass of wine. While she poured it, a young man shuffled over, half drunk, and asked me my name. His confident smile turned to a frown when he saw me as something different from what he had hoped or assumed I was. I'm used to that frown but I'm not used to aggression. When he got rowdy, the young woman talked him down, apologised, and told me to hurry home. He gets like this when he's had too much, she said. Of course she knew him. She knew all of them. They don't leave. They stay and they drink and they laugh and they fight.

Out on the dark and empty street, I saw the man again. He was standing across the way, in the sickly piss-yellow glow of an overhead streetlamp.

He crossed the road with his hands in his pockets and sighed into my face. You wouldn't have these kinds of problems, he said, if you'd just acted normal. I looked down at the ground and told him there's nothing wrong with how I am. (*I'm doing nothing more than existing*, I thought). That lad in the pub obviously thinks there's a problem, he said, a problem with you.

And who's he to say anything about me at all? I asked. At this, the man slapped a heavy hand against my shoulder. People think you're funny in the head, mate, he said too loudly and with a chuckle. He smiled but only with his mouth. His stare was serious. Angry. Upset.

Realising I didn't need to stand my ground and engage him, I said nothing else and walked away, doing my best to hold my head up and walk like nothing had bothered me at all. I felt my shoulders relax a little when I couldn't hear any footsteps coming up from behind. But just when I thought I was safe and alone again, his loud and gravelly voice filled the air all around me: *She won't be impressed*, it said.

When I arrived back at the house, it stood deathly still. I'd never entered the house after dark before, and it felt like entering a body that was holding its breath and squeezing its eyes shut.

I flicked on a light in the ground floor hall and saw her sitting on the bottom step of the stairs, her face in her hands. She was wearing that same deep red dress I had seen her in the first time.

She lifted her head and revealed a face that was made-up, but there was no sign this time that she had been crying. I was worried about you, she said, staying out so late. You don't know this village, and it doesn't like you.

I don't need your permission to go out, I said. She stood up at that, tall and imposing. So you had fun, then? she asked. You enjoyed yourself?

No, I replied. She smirked at this, then gave me a mock pout. Didn't get on with the men down at the pub? she asked, her bottom lip jutting out in a parody of sympathy. It was just the one, I explained, and he was just caught off balance because I'm new and it's a small place.

She was clearly fed up with listening to me. She walked swiftly, taking quick but decisive strides, almost instantly closing the gap between us. When she reached me, she breathed a sigh into my face, much like the man had done out on the street before. Her breath was sweeter, though, and cooler. His had been hot and wet and stale. I only want you to be safe, she said softly.

I can't always be safe, I said. The world is difficult.

You're safe here, she said, placing her hands firmly on my shoulders. She brought me in closer and embraced me, placing her warm hands against my back and pressing her chin—ever so slightly sharp—down into my shoulder.

I did nothing with my own hands but when she lifted her head and kissed me, I instinctively and gently placed my hands against her hips. Her lips were soft. She didn't hold me in place or bite down. The kiss was inviting, comforting, warming. She wanted me to enjoy it, and I did.

Eventually, she pulled away and smiled at me. She blinked slowly and looked me in the eyes. I could see that she was lost in thought for a moment, and in that moment I felt understood. Considered might be the right word.

Then she placed her thumb against my cheek and frowned, her smile suddenly vanishing, like a stain wiped away.

You have something here, she said. She rubbed her thumb

over a bump on my face. Oh, I said, it's just a skin tag or a mole. I've always had it. I shrugged. Her smile had faded but her frown deepened, making deep little grooves in her forehead, and she continued to rub her thumb over the imperfection on my cheek. She rubbed harder, and her frown harshened, until eventually she started to pick at it with her fingernails. It hurt.

I winced and told her to stop but she hushed me. She picked at it, digging the nail of her index finger into its edges and scratching. She scraped and picked and, as she went at it I watched her blink and huff and bite down on her lip in frustration.

With her other hand, she cradled and pinched the back of my neck, holding me in place with her pointed fingers and nails, and with her picking hand she dug in deeper, into the skin of this thing on my cheek. She pinched it with her sharpened nails, picked a bit off, then another, and another—chipping away at my face like a rock. Like I was an imperfect statue.

Finally, she clamped her nails down deep into what was left of the thing and tugged, like I had done with the weeds in the garden. She pulled on the blemish and I gasped and yelped and maybe screamed. Eventually, it came loose, roots and all, and I felt blood trickle freely down my cheek and over my chin.

I was crying and sweating and letting out pathetic whimpering breaths. She smiled and held out her open palm. On it was a little lump of discoloured, misshapen flesh with short, withered roots sticking out of it. It was wet with blood. She held it between her thumb and finger before suddenly popping it into her mouth like a pill. She smirked and made a show of swallowing it loudly. When she was done, I could see that specks of blood had marked her teeth.

For a moment, her eyes shimmered with a pitying look. She placed a careful hand against my arm, pecked me on the lips, and wished me goodnight before disappearing up the stairs.

February 12th, 4pm

When I woke up today, I had the feeling that so much of yesterday had been a bad dream, especially what had happened between myself and the woman when I came home last night. But the scab on my cheek and the plaster I had placed over it reminded me that it had all been very real. How was I supposed to go about my day in this house, with a man who visits often (and has taken to threatening me), and a woman who physically abuses me, leaving scars on display. Still, I've had to carry on. What else is there? To do anything else would mean giving in and showing them that I'm afraid. That, perhaps, I *deserve* to be afraid. That it's the natural order of things. And of course I am afraid, but that fact is so much less frustrating than the idea of them being satisfied in their knowledge of it.

I decided the best way to spend my day was by being as mundane as possible: coffee and toast, followed by a shower (and applying a lot of moisturiser to my increasingly sore and reddened hands), and then some tidying of the house. As I went about these things, I saw no one and heard nothing. The house was rigid and tense.

I spent time on the highest floor. Up there is a bedroom with almost nothing in it. Much like my own on the ground floor, it's sparse and there's nothing to mess up. That said, I thought the sheets might have gotten dusty over time so I decided to wash them. I carried them down to the laundry room in a basket, washed them, and hung them to dry upstairs using the radiators.

When returning to the top floor, I found a new room connected to that bedroom. I assumed it was a closet (I was looking for spare sheets and towels) but it was actually an entirely new room dedicated to sewing and tailoring.

There was a wide chest-of-drawers filled with all different fabrics: big sheets and smaller pieces of many kinds and colours. There was a desk that looked similar to the one I'm writing at right now, only it had a wood-framed, oval-shaped mirror on top of it (the kind that rotates vertically), and scattered across it were sewing tools: a pincushion, a measuring tape, spare buttons of different sizes (some plastic, others brass), a pair of scissors, spools of differently coloured threads, safety pins, and even a china thimble painted with a flower motif.

Sewing was a household chore I had always enjoyed. I'm not much of a cook at all, and despite taking on this job at this house I only clean out of necessity like anyone else does. But when a shirt is torn or a button falls off, I enjoy the little bit of creativity that goes into fixing it. I might use a coloured thread that is noticeable on purpose, sewn in with a deliberate pattern. Or I might cover the hole on a trouser leg with a patch of polka dot fabric to turn it into something new and fresh. Eye-catching.

If Catherine ever damaged something of hers, she would become so quickly disheartened. She hated the natural wear and tear that clothes endured. It frustrated her to waste money on new things, and to waste the old thing by just throwing it out even though it had been fine the day before. I always did my best to fix her things, to breathe new life into whatever the broken and worn-down thing was, whether it was a jumper or a pair of jeans. Even a single sock. Neither of us liked waste, and so I always had that opportunity to feel useful; to feel like I had accomplished something, especially if I could avoid wasting anything at all.

When we decided to go our separate ways (but remain friends), that was one thing she said she would miss about us living together. She had no patience for sewing but she also didn't want to go back to wasting money and time and things by simply and sadly throwing out stuff that could be salvaged.

I told her that she could just learn to sew, and she replied that I could just learn to cook. I laughed at that. The shoddy diet I've had since moving into this house is proof that nothing is ever as easy as we think it should be. I hate cooking, and even the disappointment that comes from eating the same few simple meals day after day can't encourage me enough to change that.

God, that's a depressing sentence to read back.

I'm sure by now Catherine has thrown out a pair of jeans and bought a new pair, and probably cursed herself as she did it. If only she had just learned how to sew. If only I had just learned how to cook.

I feel like I should mention here that the thing I've come to call my gender journey had nothing to do with our moving on from one another. Without her support, I never would have been able to dig down into myself and see what was there. She was always honest with me and it encouraged (or at least allowed) me to be honest with myself. The same goes for kindness: she was kind, and so I was able to be kind to myself, too. Sometimes. That kindness started me out on this journey. I'm not sure where it will end, if it ever does at all (there's no reason it has to), but I'm glad to be on it, and I have Catherine to thank for that. I'll always be grateful to her, for so many things.

As for what else I found in the sewing room, there was nothing out of the ordinary. A dressmaker's mannequin sat in the corner. Just a head and torso on a metal stand. It was bare but it looked used. This was a room used for grander things than just sewing buttons back on. But it also didn't have a sewing machine.

Perhaps sewing was a hobby that the occupant of this bedroom had tried to pursue, to turn into something else, once upon a time, but they never got very far. They had the space and the drive to spend some money on the necessary equipment, but failed to follow through and start making their own clothes. That was what I imagined, standing there and looking around at the dressmaking tools strewn all about.

The room was lovely, though, and I wonder if perhaps I should move myself up there (it also feels a little more isolated from the rest of the house). It's no colder on the top floor than down here, and there is a lot more light coming in. In fact, I don't think I've described this room much but it really is a dismal place. One small window, as I said, looks out onto a thin passage around the side of the house. The rest is bare walls. The floor isn't carpeted, which makes the cold more unbearable, especially when I first wake up in the morning. Now that I stop to consider it, this room is more like a cell than a bedroom. Why did I ever settle myself in here to begin with, I wonder?

I think I'll move myself upstairs.

11pm

I'm upstairs now, but moving myself up here came at a cost. Although the adrenaline has me shaking as I write, I'll try to note down everything that has happened over the course of this evening.

I was cooking my dinner for a while, spending a little extra time and effort on it. After what I wrote down earlier about being a lazy cook—and reading it back to myself—I felt like daring myself to make something more complicated. I made a mess, cleaned it up, burned things, and started again. Apparently summoned by the smell of burning, the man burst in through the back door and demanded to know what I was playing at. I told him I was cooking and that I burned something but it's fine now. He told me not to be so careless, not to waste ingredients, not to damage the pans.

I told him that I had only ruined a handful of mushrooms but he snapped, saying that they cost money, that someone had grown them and now they've gone to waste. I said I was sorry and that I'd be more careful from now on, that I was just trying something new and I'm not very experienced.

It's not me you ought to apologise to, he said.

Without making eye contact, and instead focussing on what I was making, I asked him what he wanted. He answered by closing the distance between us and standing over me. I still didn't look at him. I can do as I please, he said, it's you who needs to watch what you're doing by the looks of things.

Then, once again (for what must have been the tenth time), he asked me why I haven't made any progress with the garden. It wasn't a question at all, but a demand. I told him that I had been busy, and he scoffed. I've seen you sleeping until past noon, he said. This sent a shiver through me.

What? I asked, trying to sound as affronted and demanding as he had been. Through that window on the side path, he said. That's your room, innit? I've seen you in there fast asleep in the middle of the day. If you want to make any progress on that garden, you could start by getting up at a decent time. I told him that he had no right to watch me or judge me, and that I was about to move myself upstairs, then he wouldn't know how I spent my free time.

He took a step back into the middle of the kitchen and folded his arms tight across his barrel chest, resting them on his protruding belly. Which room? he asked. The one on the top floor, I said (silently cursing myself for bringing it up—I had no good reason for doing so, except that I was frustrated and anxious).

That's not your room, he said bluntly. I told him that my room wasn't my room either, that I had picked it at random when I first got here. I could easily have picked the top floor room when I first arrived. And good thing you didn't, he said, because it ain't yours to have.

Whose is it then? I asked. He answered by simply saying that I'd have to ask *her* if I could use that room, and he doubted she'd say yes. Then he asked me if I could sew. I said that I could and he snorted a laugh. Thought as much, he said. He closed the gap between us and mussed my hair like I was a child. Might get you to fix a few things for me then, eh?

He went back outside without a word. The day was now dark and I had no idea where he was going, but I wasn't about to ask. I was happy for his visit to have been brief, and for him to have left me alone.

I took out a bottle of white wine from the fridge and poured myself a glass. I drank it quickly, while the food finished cooking, then poured a second to have with my experimental meal.

After I finished eating, I considered packing my things up and moving them to the top floor bedroom, but the man's words rang in my ears. What would happen if I didn't ask the woman permission to move upstairs, I wondered. After what she did to my face yesterday, I was ultimately too afraid *not* to ask her.

I also thought about staying put, but that would be giving in and I didn't want that. It also meant staying in a room that he had one eye on, that he could easily invade. I had the feeling of being a caged thing at his mercy. My only choice was to ask her permission to move, and do whatever was necessary to get myself and my things upstairs and away from him.

I knocked on her door (or what I hoped was her door—I had a hard time remembering which room was which on that long corridor that stretched from one end of the house to the other. Now that I think back to this moment, though, what would have happened if I had gotten the wrong door, I wonder. There's nobody else here, surely. I've never set foot in those other rooms and I'm not likely to now, even though it's my job to check them all over and keep them in order).

When the door opened, the woman was sitting on her bed wearing a cream silk nightgown. Her curves and angles were visible underneath, giving her the appearance of a renaissance sculpture. A wave of emotions washed over me: I couldn't deny the arousal I felt, but it was mixed with an angry kind of jealousy, and those two feelings were bound together by shame. I was frustrated with myself for so many reasons, I could hardly tell them apart.

Well, she said, isn't this a nice surprise. Do you want to come in? she asked, stepping aside. I did so and she shut the door quickly. With nowhere to sit apart from on her bed (which I didn't want to do), I stood awkwardly in the middle of the room and simply blurted out my request to move up to the bedroom on the top floor of the house. In response, she placed her hands on her hips, frowned, jutted out her jaw, then crossed her arms loosely across her chest, all in the obvious performance of pretending to ponder my request.

Eventually she said: you know that's my room, yes?

Isn't this your room? I asked, gesturing to the bed. I'm using this one, she said, but the one upstairs is mine to give. It wasn't a satisfying explanation but I was in no position to argue or demand clarification. What do you want it for? she asked. I told her that my room downstairs was dank and depressing, that I wanted a warmer room with more light.

I'm happy to give you that room, she said, since I'm not currently using it. But it's going to cost you a lot. More than anything I've given you so far.

So far? I asked, suddenly feeling flushed.

The jumper, she said. That cost you a kiss. The jacket, a better kiss. And the imperfection I removed last night.

You ate that, I snapped, feeling nauseated by the memory of it. But, she said with a smile, it was for your benefit. You want to look pretty, don't you? I know you do. Once it heals, you certainly will. And I'm sure it'll heal nicely. She fluttered her eyelashes at me when I failed to say anything in return.

She smirked. You hardly wear the jumper, she said, placing her hands on her hips in mock authority. And I haven't seen you in that jacket even once. You want other things. And they will cost you so much more. She stretched the s sound, and enjoyed it. Prove to me, she said, that you want them. That you deserve them.

The heat from her bedroom instantly caused the eczema on my hands to flare up, and I used one hand to scratch at the fingers of the other. You have a rash, she said, pouting in what I took to be faux concern. It's eczema, I said. It flares up in the winter months. The air in here is dry so it's particularly itchy right now.

You shouldn't scratch it, she said, taking a step towards me and taking my hands in hers to examine them. Her features were soft, her eyes big; she wore a face of genuine concern then. I know I shouldn't, I said (finding it difficult to make much of a sound). I moisturise but sometimes the itching drives me mad.

She turned my hands over in hers, looking closely at the red bumps and dry, raw patches on my fingers and knuckles. She tutted and said that I should look after myself better. I told her that I do try my best. She said she could help me.

I know what I want in exchange for that room, she said. And it'll help you, too, to stop that nasty habit of scratching your hands. I was curious so I asked her what she wanted. I want, she said, to suck on your fingers.

She showed me a playful grin as she took one of my hands and brought it to her mouth. She tucked three of my fingers into my palm and wrapped her lips around the fourth one, sliding it deep into her mouth. She held my gaze without blinking, and I could feel her tongue dancing with the tip of my finger. She slid her mouth back and forth, blinked at me slowly, and then bit down on the first knuckle of my finger, then the second—playfully and gently. Then she bit down into the quick at the base of my fingernail. It stung.

A sharp pain went through my hand and it was an instinct to try and pull it back, but she bit down harder and slowly shook her head. *Mm-mm*, she hummed. Her front teeth were digging deeper into the soft flesh at the base of my nail, and I could feel that a little blood had escaped, which she sucked on and swallowed without opening her mouth. Her teeth dug in deeper and more blood started to run. Some escaped her lips and ran down her chin but she did nothing to wipe it away. I squirmed like a child and tears blurred my vision. I asked her to stop, begged her, even cried out, but she remained so calm and still, clamping her teeth down harder and harder, deeper and deeper into the quick of my first finger.

I started to panic, just as I had done the night before, and just like then there was nothing I could think to do to escape, save for lashing out at her, which I wouldn't do.

My whimpering grew louder and I could feel my legs turning to jelly, and then it was over. She pulled with her teeth, and my fingernail came loose at the roots. When she at last let go of my finger, I let out a groan and held it up to the light to see that my nail was completely gone. The fresh, red skin beneath it was exposed to the air, and felt cold and sharp.

She flashed me a full set of teeth, my bloodied fingernail clamped between them. Then she let out a throaty chuckle, and swallowed the thing whole.

I wiped the tears from my eyes with the heels of my hands, and avoided the temptation to suck the blood from my fresh fingertip. She showed me another performative pout and placed a hand against my cheek. She jutted out her bottom lip and said aw as she rubbed her thumb softly against my skin. She was mocking me, but I didn't stop her.

I wasn't sure what happened next. I felt paralysed by choice; despite the only choice, in retrospect, being to leave without a word and find something to bandage my hand with. But I didn't do that. I looked at her, searching for any reason why she would do something like that to me. The question must have been written across my face because she said to me then: now you won't be able to scratch so easily. But we're certainly not done.

She held out her flat palm, obviously expecting me to place my other hand in it for her to do the same again. I recoiled at the idea, clutching my hands to my chest and resisting the urge to cry again. At this, she rolled her eyes and asked me if it was really half as bad as I was making it out to be. I paused to consider the pain in my hand and found that it was, indeed, minimal. The bleeding had stopped quickly and the sensation of bare, fresh skin against the cool air was odd, but there was truthfully very little pain in it at all. There had been, at first, but only a few moments later it had swiftly simmered away.

As though she fully knew the answer already—as though she knew exactly how much it would and did hurt (or didn't)—she gestured for me to surrender my other hand, and so I did, without hesitation. She held it gently in hers, our fingers touching softly. She stroked my palm with her fingertips and it tickled. The sensation danced on that line between pleasure and irritation, and I let out a childlike chuckle that I am embarrassed about now, but in the moment she offered me a genuine, delighted smile at the sound of it.

She brought my hand to her mouth and, once again, wrapped her lips tight around my finger.

She did the same thing again, sucking on my finger, playing with it using her tongue and teeth, before eventually biting down on the sensitive, supple layer of flesh around the base of my fingernail, and pulling it away.

It felt easier this time, and faster. Being wiser to what was coming should have made it harder to bear, and much more frightening. I should have felt so much anxiety, but I didn't. The nervousness I did feel was more like butterflies in my stomach than trepidation and upset. I felt a ridiculous urge to giggle, like I was doing something naughty that I might get in trouble for, rather than something which anyone else might rightly call unnatural.

When it was done, I felt better; still glad that it was over but mostly proud of myself for having gotten through it (twice, at that). Once again, as before, the bleeding soon stopped and the pain faded as quickly as it had come.

You can have the bedroom, she said. It's yours. She smiled from ear to ear.

When I started writing this entry, I was shaking, but reliving the experience in order to get it down on paper has me feeling aroused and confused and proud and ashamed.

February 13th, 12pm

I woke up early. Or I should more accurately say that I was awoken early by the sun shining in. When Catherine and I lived together, this was a point of contention for us both. I have always loved being woken up by the sun. I'm not an early bird, but the idea of being kissed awake by the morning light has always been a romantic one for me. It's a lovely way to start the day. It has never failed to set me off in a good mood. Even if I have only slept a few hours, I've always felt that I would have a good day if the sun woke me up naturally. Who doesn't enjoy being woken up by bright, warm sunlight?

At least, that's what I always felt. Catherine hated it, though, and wanted to install blackout curtains in every place we ever lived. Fortunately for me, we moved around too much for that to ever be possible. Perhaps that's selfish of me. Actually, it surely is, but it wasn't me selfishly putting my foot down that stopped it from happening; only practicality and cost.

I could finally have this every day now, though. Being woken up by the sun after around seven or eight hours of sleep is the perfect way to start my day, and that's just how today began. And that meant no laying in bed lazily wanking my morning wood and then spending too long in the shower. I got up happily, tied my hair into a messy bun, shaved at the sink instead of in the shower (as I had done since first setting foot in this house) and headed downstairs to make breakfast and have some coffee.

The house was still. I prepared and ate a quick breakfast in peace. Then I took myself into the garden to see what could be done out there. It took me until then to look at the state of my two index fingers. It occurred to me to wear gloves to avoid any potential infection, but I hadn't thought to look at them in any detail until then because there had been no pain at all. I found that I had no particularly strong feelings about what had happened the night before, and so I slipped on some gardening gloves and tended to the weeds as I had done so many times before.

It hit me then that I should perhaps go out and buy some seeds. Maybe a few new flowers and plants would be just the thing to stave off and fight back the weeds. Maybe they were always coming back because they had room to grow. Fresh flowers could solve that, surely. Tomorrow, I'll go out and buy some packets of seeds.

Actually, no. I'll pop out now and get some. No time like the present.

4pm

The man was in the garden when I came back.

I wasn't gone long, honestly. I had put on a little makeup to go out, but I hadn't bothered to change into anything nicer. I knew I wouldn't be gone long.

When I got back, he was kneeling beside a flower bed, pulling up a few weeds. The first thing I saw was his wide backside, faded blue jeans stretched across it, and a patch of greying back hair poking out from under his hiked-up polo shirt (it was usually tucked into his jeans, stretched painfully taut over his bulging belly).

He soon sensed I was there, or perhaps he heard me, and when he brought his heavy frame to its feet he turned to me and smirked. So you're back, he said. I saw that you were out here before so I came to give you a hand, but then you were gone.

You saw that I was out here? I asked. When he didn't reply, I simply moved past it: I went to get seeds, I said. For what? he asked. For the garden, I said, to fill up all the empty spaces and fight back against the weeds.

He let out something like a sigh and a laugh mixed together

and folded his arms. That's not—he groaned—how you get rid of weeds. That wouldn't work at all, would it? If you thought about it for five seconds.

Well, I said, I've been applying weed killer and pulling them out at the root. I thought I'd try something different. He slapped his meaty, calloused hands together to get some of the dirt off them. Clumped bits of black and brown fell to the ground. You gotta keep at it, he said, examining his own leathery hands—dirt caked into the creases—that's the only way.

He stepped towards me and frowned. This was the first time he had properly looked at me. He squinted his eyes and screwed up his mouth. Are you wearing *makeup*? he asked. I nodded. Why? he asked. I shrugged and said with a forced smile: Why aren't you?

This was a retaliation I had used once before with someone else, and it had caused them to stumble over their own reply. I thought (hoped) it might work again here. It didn't. He snorted and re-crossed his arms. Because I'm not a girl, he said proudly. And neither are you. And if you want to help me deal with these weeds, you're going to go and wash that shit off first, then pass me the bottle of weed killer and we can deal with this properly.

I don't want to help you, I said. I want to take care of this garden by myself. He snapped at this. There was no time between him tossing out mockery and aggression, and him throwing a heavy punch at me.

It connected with my cheek and I stumbled backwards onto

my arse. I had never been hit before and I was shocked by how much it hurt. There was a throbbing in my bruised bones and a stinging in my skin where it had ripped clean open. My eyes welled up quickly and I started sniffing and huffing and panting and grunting. So many noises; it was pathetic.

You ungrateful little shit, he muttered through gritted teeth. I'm out here spending my free time happily helping you when I could be doing *anything else*, and that's what you say to me? He put his balled-up hands to his hips and sighed, bowing his head in a show of exasperation, then started pacing like a caged animal.

Unbelievable, he said at last. He seemed genuinely offended. I almost felt bad for a moment, like I should perhaps apologise and tell him that I did need his help after all. Instead, I got to my feet and kept quiet, waiting to see what he would say next.

In the end, after huffing and puffing for a few moments, all he said was: Fine, if that's how you want it to be. He raised up his hands in mock defeat (like he was being arrested) and marched into the house with a deep frown drawn across his face, slamming the door behind him as he went.

As a show of defiance, however small and pathetic, I stayed out in the garden and went about weeding and planting a few new seeds. The cut on my cheek bled freely as I continued, and I occasionally had to wipe away fresh blood until the bleeding stopped. As I stopped and gazed around, the garden seemed clearer and cleaner than I'd ever seen it. That might have been thanks to his work but I'm not about to entertain that thought. This is my work.

11pm

I didn't see the woman today, and the immediate disappointment that I felt surprised me.

Her removing my nails had worked to stop the bad habit of scratching at my knuckles and wrists, where my eczema is always at its worst. Even though I still had eight other nails to scratch with, the constant reminder that two were missing was enough to jar me out of scratching at all each and every time I moved to do so. Whenever I went to scratch and felt the soft nub of my first fingertip press uselessly against the dry bits of skin on my hands, I instead reached for my moisturiser and applied that instead. It was working.

In the bathroom earlier, I had stared at my own face in the mirror and inspected the slowly healing scar that replaced the blemish she had so violently removed. It was already clear that, once it fully healed (which I'm sure it would), I would have a perfectly smooth face. Both cheeks would be clear, soft, and without so much as a freckle.

February 14th, 10am

Today is Valentine's Day. The only reason I know is because of this journal. In fact, without my daily writing, I wouldn't have a clue what the date was at all.

Catherine and I didn't celebrate Valentine's Day. Not really. We felt the pressure of it—this feeling that we should do something or other; that if we didn't, well, we were just being miserable to each other, and dull worst of all. So, we would buy each other a present (nothing romantic; just something the other would like), then have a fun day out somewhere or maybe go to see a play. We would never have dinner out, though. The thought of being a couple in a restaurant full of other couples made her feel queasy, and I didn't really like the idea of it much either.

This has me wondering what we did for our last Valentine's Day together. I'm not even sure where in the world we were, but we must have given each other a small gift and done something nice. How strange I don't remember now. But the thought that this same day, only one year ago, must have been a much happier day than today will surely be… it has me feeling very low all of a sudden.

Looking out the window, there's nothing at all to see. Today is grey layered upon grey. The sky is like a flat, floating slab of concrete suspended over rolling hills that stretch out into the distance; they look as though the colour has been bled from them, sucked up into that oppressive sky. A good excuse, I suppose, for not doing any more work in the garden today. For not doing much of anything, perhaps.

1pm

I have decided to bring my journal to the cafe and write here. The day is so grey and my memories (or lack thereof) from last year have brought me so low. I feel like I can barely lift my head at all. On days like this, staying in the house is something I can't stand to do. I have to go somewhere else, eat food made by someone else, buy myself something. I've brought a book with me as well: a novel by a woman who died from a cold she caught at her own brother's funeral.

It's the same girl working behind the counter as the last time I came in, making the coffee and serving the cakes and pastries. Maybe she owns the cafe. We had a nice exchange as I ordered myself a coffee and a slice of carrot cake, which I savoured slowly while reading. One bite per page.

The man has just come into the cafe.

10pm

When she took my nails, the pain was brief. This time, the thing she has done to me hurts so much more, and the bleeding still hasn't stopped, even as I write this now. My head is foggy and my eyes are stinging from the tears, which also won't stop, dammit. Let me go back.

I'll start with the man. He came into the cafe without ordering anything and sat down at my table. I can't say whether or not he knew he would find me there. He didn't look surprised to see me, but I just don't know. When he sat down he sighed through his nose like a dog and jutted out his jaw. Eventually he told me to show him my hands. When I did, he scowled and bit down hard on his lip with an entire row of teeth.

You let her do that to you? he asked me. I nodded. He sighed through his nose again before asking me: Why can't you sort out your own problems?

She offered, I said. I did my best to look him in the eye. It was in exchange for the room, I added. You told me she wouldn't let me have it so I gave her my nails. You let her do that to you, he repeated (it wasn't a question this time), a look of disgust on his face. Have some self respect. Are you a boy or a man?

When I told him I was neither, he told me not to be cheeky and struck me across the face with the back of his hand. He didn't think about it before doing it. It was an entirely automatic reaction to what I had said; a natural consequence. I speak, he slaps. It's how the world works.

I felt all the anger in me rise up and spill over in a single moment. I got to my feet, not entirely sure what I expected myself to do (*It'll be a nice surprise*, I thought). When he followed my lead and towered several inches above me, I was too shaken in the moment to care for feeling intimidated by someone larger than myself, and I grabbed at the front of his polo shirt with one hand and threatened to punch him with the other (I balled it up tight, ready to strike, to show that it was not an empty threat).

He smirked and dared me to do it, so I did.

I've never punched anyone before, and it felt wonderful. My knuckles were stinging and the bones in my fingers were throbbing, but I was so excited. My skin prickled with the sheer pleasure of it. I didn't care about the pain or the consequences. I was almost giddy to have finally done the thing I had secretly fantasised about doing for (what felt like) so long.

I left him grunting and snorting and rubbing at his face like an ape, but soon enough he followed me out of the cafe. I turned back towards him so as not to be taken off-guard. It didn't help.

He was on me in a moment; he put one hand on my shoulder and punched me in the gut with the other. It hurt so much I couldn't stand back up after I dropped to the concrete. When I eventually caught my breath and lifted my head, he was gone. I wondered if this was the kind of injury a doctor should look at, but after walking around the village for a while to calm myself down and find my breath, the aching had eased and I retreated back to the house.

When I entered the foyer through the main door, she was waiting there for me, just as she had been that time before. This time, she was bathed in natural light in spite of the grey of the day. She gave me a pitiful look, as though I were a child that had scraped its knees.

She cocked her head to one side and pouted (this time, somehow with more honesty than she had in the past). Then at last she invited me into her arms. I hugged her tight without giving it a thought. After holding me for a long while, she took both my hands in hers, held them close to her chest, and kissed me. It was a soft, warm kiss. The kind of kiss that lovers share.

She let go of one hand and lifted the other to the light, inspecting my sore and red knuckles. Does it still hurt? she asked. I shook my head. Good, she said with a smile. Come with me, brave boy.

I didn't correct her.

She took me to her bedroom and locked the door behind us. At the foot of her bed was a metal tray, and on it were several plates of freshly-cooked food. So many of my favourite things. We sat on the bed like two little children—our legs crossed—and ate together quietly. She laughed when I smeared my chin with sauce, and even dropped some on my jumper. She lifted it up over my head and off me and said not to worry, that she would wash it happily. We ate two desserts each: a slice of cake and a bowl of ice cream. It was sweet and indulgent and I felt soothed by it all. I felt a little strength return to my tired, aching bones.

There was a warmth in the room that filled the air and crept over my skin and spread through my veins. I felt so much in that moment.

After she removed the tray of plates and bowls, she came back to the bed and sat close beside me, her robe draped over her in a way that seemed at once careless and perfectly considered, revealing the parts of her she wanted revealed. She took my hand in hers, just as she had done before, when she took my nails. This time she asked me: do you want me to get rid of him?

The man? I asked. She nodded and smiled with only her lips. What would that mean? I asked. When she didn't answer me, I asked her another question: what is your relationship to him, exactly? She paused to chew on the question, almost literally (she seemed to be grinding her teeth). Eventually, she chuckled as though remembering a joke, and simply said that he is useful to her.

He is cruel, I said. She nodded at that with the same empty smile. The expression on her face told me that she was very aware of what he was, but that she also simply accepted it. Why haven't you gotten rid of him before now? I asked.

Like I said (she squeezed my hand here suddenly), he is useful.

So, I said, why now? She grinned, showing me her lovely teeth. I'll do it for you, she said, happily.

I didn't understand, but I did want the man to go away. It all seemed too easy, though. I wonder this now, and I wondered it then. It would be so easy for him to just disappear. He had come to feel like a challenge to me. I had faced up to him earlier, and I almost wanted a chance to do it again. But then, I had already done it, I had nothing left to prove to him or to myself or to her, and who was to say how much worse he would become after today. So, I agreed. I asked her what she wanted.

I laughed first, to make her think that I might be joking, and then I said: How about my testicles? You can take those.

She laughed, too, much louder and harder and more genuinely than I had done. I continued to smile, but asked her with as much nonchalance as I could manage: Why not? Because, she said (she was still laughing) I like them. I might like to use them. She fluttered her eyelashes at me then. I felt my penis stiffen at that, and this absent reaction led to so much frustration that I squeezed my hand into a fist.

How about these, she said, placing a hand against my ribs and rubbing her thumb over my nipple. It hardened immediately. They're useless, anyway, she added, continuing to rub it. Why keep something that serves no purpose at all to you.

I liked my nipples. I liked having them played with, just as she was doing then. But she was right: they did nothing of use. Now, though, I wonder if I thought that because I simply wanted to agree with her. I wanted to see her point. I wasn't sure who or what I would be without them, though, and that frightened me.

I can't make this decision now, I said. I need to think. But she shook her head and said no, no time to think.

I want them, she said.

I liked the way she said that, and in that moment I wanted her to be happy, to be satisfied. And so I removed my t-shirt.

Sitting there with nothing on my top half, I felt exposed and vulnerable. I felt like a child. *Adults don't sit half-dressed*, I thought.

She placed her hand just as it had been before, rubbing my nipple with her thumb until it hardened. She traced her thumb about its outside, giving me goosebumps across my bare chest.

She giggled when I shivered, and pressed down on my nipple like she was curious about it, like it was a new toy that she wanted to play with. She pinched it between her thumb and finger, and pulled on it, and smiled. Then she let go, placed her hands on my shoulders, and lowered me gently onto my back, my head against the pillow.

Once again, she teased my nipple (just the one, not the other). She tickled it with her fingertip and rubbed her thumb over it softly. Then she moved her other hand down to my crotch and slid it into my trousers. Taking my stiff penis firmly in her hand, she leaned her head down and began sucking on my nipple.

She played with my penis, rubbing her thumb over its head and pulling slowly up and down, and at the same time she sucked loudly on my nipple. She moaned as she did this (like she was enjoying it even more than I was), gnawing and licking and sucking on it. She teased my penis in the most frustrating way, not tugging on it aggressively or with purpose but just playing for her own amusement. It drove me to frustration, and all the while she was lost in her own fun as she chewed on my nipple and licked at it with the tip of her tongue. A thin trail of saliva slithered down my chest, over my ribs, and onto the bed.

Then she bit down hard, suddenly and without warning. At the same time, she gripped too tightly onto my penis and squeezed. She sank her teeth into the edges of my areola, grunting as she did so.

She continued to drool over my chest, and it felt as though her teeth were searching for purchase, something to grip onto. She dug them deeper into my flesh until, at last, she pierced my skin and I felt my blood flow free. She started to move her hand again, this time with purpose. She tugged on my penis furiously, up and down, quickly and steadily.

Her teeth had sunk so deep into my skin, they dug under my nipple. She closed her jaw tight and began to pull. I let out an enormous, unrestrained scream, the tears streaming down my face.

In response, she only pulled harder and faster on my penis and it continued to feel good. My body was on fire, feeling everything all at once: the highest pleasure and the deepest pain. The blood flowed in little rivers over my chest and in all directions. I felt some reach my neck, some snake down to my belly. All the while she tugged and her sharp teeth dug into my flesh and her hand pumped up and down under my clothes.

I felt something come loose, something tear and snap. And at the same time, my penis started to twitch. The final snap happened as I exploded over her fingers. She pulled her head and hand away at the same time and I felt a relief I had never experienced in my life.

The relief was brief, though, and soon replaced by a sharp pain that wouldn't stop. There was a gaping wound in my chest and the blood continued to flow.

The pleasure I had experienced numbed the initial eruption of pain, but when that pleasure passed (as it always does), the pain remained, and I screamed and I cried. Through blurred eyes I saw her chew on and swallow the chunk of flesh she had ripped from me. She smiled and, even though I grunted and whimpered and sobbed, she asked me softly if I was ready to go again.

I shook my head but couldn't keep my eyes open. I squeezed them tight and begged for the hot pain and the bleeding to stop. In the whirlwind of pain and fear, and through the sound of blood pumping in my ears, I still heard her giggle. I found enough strength to be angry at her, but soon it was pushed aside to make room for more pain and more anxiety. I must take the other one, she said, or else this will all have been for nothing. You wanted him gone, but he won't go anywhere at all if I don't get everything that you promised I could have.

Feeling drunk on the pain, dizzy and disorientated, I slid off the bed and onto shaking, unsteady feet. My knees buckled and I fell onto all fours. Blood dripped onto the carpet.

After pushing myself back up, I kept one hand pressed against the hole in my chest (though I could barely stand to touch it, but I had to try and stop the bleeding), and staggered out of the room. She let me go without either of us saying a word.

In the bathroom, I found everything I needed to disinfect and bandage my wound. The bleeding wasn't bad enough to frighten me, but it also wouldn't stop (in the time that I've been writing, I think it finally has). As I bound my chest, I swear I could hear the guffawing noise of the man's laughter outside the bathroom, but it may have been nothing at all, only my imagination playing cruel tricks. When I stumbled back up to this room, my ears ringing and my head spinning, I saw and heard nobody at all.

February 15th, 12pm

When I woke up, the man was in my room.

He was sitting in this chair, watching and waiting for me to wake up. When I did, and saw him, my heart started racing so quickly it hurt. It made the wound in my chest ache.

He smiled without showing any teeth, and got slowly to his feet by pressing his open hands against his knees and grunting. Each knee clicked and popped twice. He walked over to my bed and stood over me, that pinched smile still painted across his face. You see this? he asked. He pointed one thick finger to his cheek, the skin of which was swollen and slightly redder than that of the other, with flecks of purple mixed into the red. You did this, he said. Did it feel good?

Yes, I thought, *of course it did*, but I couldn't say that. And so I said nothing. On any other morning, I might have been tempted to get out of bed, ignore my nerves, and take another swing at him. Perhaps that's just bravado talking, because I was in too much pain to try.

He grabbed my duvet and pulled it away from me, leaving my half-naked body exposed and pathetic-looking. He frowned at the botched bandaging across my chest, the bloodstains, and then he snorted and smirked. He must have known what had happened. But how much did he know? Did he know the deal I made with her, and that the deal didn't go through? Did he know my thoughts? What about hers?

How connected were they? What did they share?

He took me by the wrist and lifted me up. I was forced onto my feet, to stand in front of him. I wrapped both arms across my chest, hugging my shoulders. He let out the same snort in response to that. Look at you, he said.

Then he struck me across the face with the back of his hand. I kept my balance. You wanna hit me, don't you? he asked. Go on, then.

I didn't. I thought that if I stood there and did nothing at all, he would get bored and leave. Instead, he poked at my bandages with one thick finger and I let out a pained, sad sound. He chuckled at that. He moved to slowly peel the tape back and expose the wound. I grabbed at his wrist to stop him, and the look of satisfaction on his face—satisfaction over getting some kind of response out of me—was enough to boil my blood. I felt my skin turn hot and prickly. He looked me in the eye and grinned. I could see the cogs turning behind his eyes. He ruffled my hair, told me to get it cut, and left without saying another word. The lack of satisfaction was itchy and irritating. It would have felt better if he had knocked me out.

February 16th, 11am

Yesterday, after the man had intruded on and violated my space and my body, I decided to go over every room in the house as quickly as possible, cleaning and tidying and airing it all out.

The day was nice, the sky clear; a cool breeze was blowing. I couldn't do much physical exertion with how much my wound was hurting, and occasionally I thought about how one of my nipples had been ripped away and eaten. It would make me feel dizzy and nauseated every time I stopped to picture it, but I would still just continue with my sorting and dusting and do my best to push it all away.

I washed every beige surface in the bathroom and cleaned every stained appliance in the kitchen. I made the sinks sparkle. The room filled with filing cabinets had been upended somehow: files scattered and stacks of paper knocked to the floor. Either the wind or the man was to blame, I thought, but it didn't matter. It gave me something to do. Though it did take longer to fix that room than I would have liked, and bending down to gather up the pages was nothing less than agony for my chest. Each time I bent down, I feared reopening the wound in my chest. I was careful, of course, but there's only so careful you can be.

I went back down to my old bedroom. The air was musty and tasted of dust. I drew the curtains and opened the one tiny window to air it out, then dusted every surface and changed the bedsheets.

When I was happy with the state of the room, I moved to leave but found the door locked. Turning the latch did nothing at all. Panic set fire to my skin as I started to tug with all my weight, pressing against the frame, but still it didn't budge. Soon enough I heard faint laughter on the other side of the door. It grew louder. And then the footsteps. I knew it was him. Of course it was him. Who else could be so spiteful and petty. He let out a raspy guffaw with a pathetic hollowness. What's wrong? he shouted from the other side. Locked yourself in, have you?

I didn't reply but continued to try the latch and pull on the handle. I slapped and punched at the door, then before I knew it I was grunting and shouting like something caged and angry. I punched at the wood with a closed fist, but that did far more damage to myself. Eventually, as I gave the handle another tug, it flung open and sent me tumbling backwards to the floor. The pain was made so much worse by my chest wound.

I composed myself as quickly as possible, knowing that he was standing in the doorway, laughing and judging me. I got to my feet and did my best to hide the pain and the humiliation. I didn't hesitate. I threw myself at him, throwing punches that missed. He took hold of my wrists and pulled me in close. A big man, are you? He cackled before throwing me back across the threshold. I could lock you in again, y'know, he threatened. He was smiling while I continued to grunt and puff. He was enjoying it and I didn't know how to stop him. Just like before, he walked away without another word.

I didn't know what else to do except keep working, so I spent the rest of the afternoon moving from room to room. Last place was the basement, which I had never tidied because I hated spending time down there. With no natural light, there was never an ideal time of day to spend in the basement. But when you've had to fight off real threats, imagined fears and discomforts don't even register, so I went down there without a thought. I boxed up a few old and broken things: parts of machines that were rusted and belonged to nothing; torn and discarded bits of clothing; things so ruined by water damage that I couldn't tell what they had once been. I organised the detergents, threw out old bottles, and dusted the floor. It was the best I could do in an airless and half-dark room.

Finally, I went out into the garden. I found the man on his knees, hard at work, and when he heard me come out he got to his feet and shook his head. Oh no, he said, no no no, get the fuck out, this is my garden. This is my work. You don't touch any of this.

I once again reminded him that this house was my responsibility, that the garden was mine to tend, and that I enjoyed the work. He wiped the mud from his bare hands on his jeans, clenched his fists, and marched over to me, his face purple and a spew of angry words spilling from his mouth. I stopped him with a kick to his crotch. I'd had all I could bear.

I stood over him and watched as he dropped to his knees and crumpled like a ball of paper. He covered his crotch with both hands. Every bit of exposed skin had turned red. He was groaning like a wounded animal. He looked so fragile.

I should have run away, locked myself in my bedroom, done anything other than what I did, which was to just stand tall and feel proud. He was down there for a while, but he didn't get back up slowly. As soon as he found his strength, he used every bit of it getting to his feet and grabbing me with both hands. He wrapped them around my throat and squeezed.

When I woke up, it was dark. The sky was punctured with little pinpricks of light and the moon was full. Despite being awake, my arms and legs felt drained and deflated. I imagined myself lying there until dawn.

Then she came. I heard her soft footsteps crunching the grass nearby, and then her silhouetted head blocking out the moon, forming a slight halo of silver light around her. She tutted and tsked, called me a poor baby, and asked if I could sit up. I told her I didn't have the strength and she tutted again. I couldn't make out her expression but I imagined she was pouting in mock sympathy.

Is it too late? I asked her.

For what, dear?

For you to get rid of him, I said.

Not at all.

She said nothing else, slipped my t-shirt off me, and sank her teeth into my chest without warning. She offered me no pleasure, no distraction, but I didn't need it. As soon as her teeth broke through my skin and my blood started to flow, I placed one hand on the back of her head and stroked her hair. With the other hand, I fingered the cold grass. I plucked out individual blades and rolled them between my fingers. I dug my fingertips into the dirt and felt the soft moistness of it. I heard the sound of her licking up my blood, and the sound of bits of me ripping and coming apart. Eventually, she pulled her head back and blocked out the moon again. In the glow of it I could see her wipe the blood from her chin, chew on the thing in her mouth, and swallow.

I must have passed out after that. I try to think if anything else happened but, if it did, it's lost. I woke up to the sound of birds and the sun on my face. I was still on the lawn, half naked and with an exposed wound on my chest. It ached as I sat up. Clumps of dried blood had crusted against my skin like barnacles. I dared not touch the wound, but at least it had stopped bleeding.

When I took myself inside, the house was silent and still. Not like a held breath, but like a thing quietly sleeping. I showered carefully but thoroughly, scratching off the dried blood from my chest. Then I bandaged the new wound and redressed the old one. I would need to go out and buy new bandages and some pills for the pain. Though, in truth, I don't feel much of it at all. There was a dull ache, a soreness, but not much more.

6pm

After making myself lunch, I went out to get more bandages and painkillers, took just one, then stopped at the cafe for a cup of coffee. I sat and nursed it as I thought over what had transpired last night. She and I had spoken so little. I had asked her to do what she did. I gave her permission. I wanted her to do it. Now there is less of me, but I feel comfortable. Comforted.

Back home, I walked from room to room and checked the state of each. Everything was in a pleasant order. Even the kitchen was tidy, its floor clean. I looked out the kitchen window and saw the garden empty.

The weeds had been calmed and mostly removed. There was space for everything to breathe. It's still too early in the year for anything to bloom, but give it another month and things will. Maybe I should prune a few of the bushes and plants. I'll look up how to do it later and give it a go tomorrow.

I made an early dinner, my appetite being particularly strong today, and took another painkiller.

11pm

After I ate, I went looking for her. I didn't really think about doing so—it was almost automatic. I found her room on that long corridor, and when I knocked I got no answer. I went inside and the bed was perfectly made, draped with a wool blanket and with a row of cushions placed on top of the pillows at the head. But she wasn't there.

I moved about the room, looking for things that would tell me more about her. I pulled open the drawers as softly as I could and found them full of what you'd expect: fresh sheets, ironed and folded; one small drawer full of underwear and another of socks and tights and stockings. I rummaged through her dish of jewellery, took out a necklace and held it against my chest, admiring it in the mirror. I tucked my hair to one side and put the necklace on.

Her wardrobe was impressive. She had shown it to me once before but now I was taking it all in by myself, slowly and with admiration. I took a red lace dress from its hanger and checked it against myself to see if it would fit, then I took off my shirt and trousers and tried it on. It fit like a glove, even fitting my hips and waist perfectly. I felt satisfied. Then she came in.

She saw me in the dress and the necklace, and she asked me what I was doing. I apologised for trying them on without her permission, explained that I couldn't seem to resist, and asked her if she thought I looked nice in them. I hoped that the question came off as playful, but her face remained stern and unmoving as a brick wall. It was horrible to look at, and I felt that she thought the same about me.

Take it all off, she said. I did, without a word.

She closed the gap between us and placed a soft hand against my bare chest, between the bandages. If you want—she said slowly—to wear something like that, you must give me more of you.

How much more? I asked. So much more, she said. How much more did I want to give, I wondered, and how much would I have left of me after she was done. I wanted to be beautiful in the dress and the necklace. If I kept giving her bits of me, I could never be beautiful. But was it beauty that I was really after? Or was it something else? I didn't have answers. I also didn't want to give up on what I wanted, on whatever it was that I was inexorably drawn to, on what should have been so simple and easy to obtain. But then, she had given me so much already, I should want to thank her and show her my gratitude.

As though she could read my thoughts, see them swirling like clouds above my head, she smiled and went to the wardrobe. She retrieved a hanger holding a black suit with three buttons on the jacket, and an ironed white shirt. Put this on, she said.

Why? I asked.

If you put these on, she said with a sigh, you won't have to give me any more of you.

I took the suit from her and held it out in front of me. After taking a moment to think, and then another, I lowered the suit and looked her in the eye. I think, I said, I want to give you more of me.

Really? she asked. She looked genuinely surprised.

Don't you want more of me? I asked. She nodded. I'll let you wear the dress, and my jewellery, and sew nice things in the little room upstairs.

I liked the sound of that, and so I dropped the suit and took myself over to the bed. I lay my body down and she sat softly beside me. She draped her hair over one shoulder and bowed her head forward to kiss, bite, and chew on me.

CHLOE.CLAIRE1

Comment from @Chloe.Claire1:
Oh, this review made my heart sing! I struggle so much with sensory overload these days but this movie sounds like something I could certainly handle. I'll make sure to check it out as soon as possible. Thank you so much for your video!

Reply from @FilmFanFaye:
Thank you so much! Glad you enjoyed the video :)

Comment from @Chloe.Claire1:
Wow, you really captured what this movie seems to be saying. You have such a wonderful passion for filmmaking and the people who create films. I sometimes have trouble connecting emotionally with the characters in a movie, but it's always the themes that tug so harshly at my heart in the most beautiful ways possible. The themes of this one—loneliness, isolation, rejection—are all ones I understand on a deeply personal level. Please keep making these wonderful, joyous videos.

Reply from @FilmFanFaye:
I really appreciate your comment, thank you! I'm glad the themes of this movie speak to you, but I'm also sorry that you relate so much to such dark themes. I hope you have a great day :)

Reply from @Chloe.Claire1:
Yes, I've had a difficult life, especially during my childhood and for the past few years. But I appreciate you taking the time to reply to my comment. You're very sweet and thoughtful, Faye, thank you!

Comment from @Chloe.Claire1:
Oh! Another movie review so soon! You work so hard, and your fans are all very grateful, I'm sure! I saw this film many years ago and it left a real impact on me. I still viscerally recall the scene where the rabbit gets injured. It is almost burned onto the backs of my eyelids and I still see it when I close my eyes.

Reply from @FilmFanFaye:
It is a very impactful scene, I agree. Sorry it had that much of a strong effect on you. While I do believe in a filmmaker's right to freely create art uninhibited, I also spend a lot of time thinking about the emotional impact of scenes the audience never saw coming, and how we just can't let go of them.

Reply from @Chloe.Claire1:
Yes, that's exactly it! Oh Faye, you put it so well, so eloquently indeed! How are we to know what scenes we will come across, what moments will speak to us, what images will stay with us forever, maybe even damaging us in the long-term? It is impossible to say, but I do believe that good art is important to consume and enjoy, even if it sometimes hurts us in much the same way that a loved one can hurt us.

Reply from @FilmFanFaye:
I certainly don't disagree, Chloe, but please also make sure to look after yourself.

Reply from @Chloe.Claire1:
You're very sweet to think of me, thank you!

Comment from @Chloe.Claire1:
Goodness, Faye, you really put so much into this video. A list of movies like this one must have taken so much time and care to compile, and yet you still poured such love and attention into each choice, each summary, each opinion. Your viewers are very appreciative. I haven't seen the film that took the top spot because I'm far too afraid of horror movies these days. They have such a frightening and painful impact on me. I can feel them in my chest. I worry so much that my heart could stop when I watch them. But perhaps, if you feel so passionately about this one, I should do my best to watch and enjoy and appreciate it.

Reply from @FilmFanFaye:
Please don't watch any movie that is going to do you any kind of damage. We all have our genres and styles that we prefer and you don't need to upset yourself just to watch a film. Have a great day!

Reply from @Chloe.Claire1:
Oh, thank you so much for your concern, for worrying about me. You are incredibly sweet. I wish I had someone like you in my life to look after me and always consider my wellbeing. I will still consider watching the movie, but it might take me some time to emotionally prepare for my viewing experience. We will see.

Reply from @FilmFanFaye:
Okay well please just take care. Horror movies aren't for everyone.

Reply from @Chloe.Claire1:
I certainly will do my best to take care, Faye. It's not always

easy for me, and there are certainly things far beyond my control, sadly. But I will look after myself so that I can continue to watch your wonderful videos, and the great movies that you continue to review and recommend. Thank you so much for what you do for us all.

———··•··———

Comment from @Chloe.Claire1:
You speak so eloquently about the topic of film and media. It's clear to me that you have both knowledge and passion, and these things simply radiate from you as you speak. However, I'm sorry to say that I don't think I'll be able to sit through this movie either. The moments of domestic abuse which you mentioned would hit far too close to home for me. My mother was not kind to me as a child, and she remains frightening and intimidating to this very day. Watching such a movie, I fear, would trigger some dark memories for me which I am so afraid to dig up. I hope you don't mind that I won't be watching this one. I so wish to see things the way that you do, and to appreciate all the same art that you love to talk about and share with us all!

Reply from @FilmFanFaye:
I mentioned to someone else in the comments of a previous video that we don't have to get upset by forcing ourselves to watch certain films. I believe that good art should challenge us, but you need to look after yourself first.

Reply from @Chloe.Claire1:
Yes, that person was me, and I do know that you are right. But I so dislike having to miss out on certain important pieces of cinema because of my own fears and traumas. It makes me feel like a failure and I don't want to fail.

Reply from @FilmFanFaye:
I don't think you're a failure. Treat yourself with kindness, Chloe :)

Reply from @Chloe.Claire1:
Oh Faye, thank you so much for your kind words and your patience. You treat me ever so sweetly, and I can't tell you just how much I appreciate it. You shine so brightly that you have become a light for me in the darkness. Thank you so very much. Have a beautiful day.

———··●··———

Chloe.Claire1 started following you.

———··●··———

Chloe.Claire1: Hello dear Faye. I hope you don't mind me following you on here and reaching out in a direct message, but I am so enamoured with your tastes and the ways in which you share great film recommendations with us all across your platforms. You do such wonderful work and I hope to support you wherever and however I can.

FilmFanFaye: Hey Chloe, thanks for the follow. I always enjoy connecting with other film fans :) It means a lot that you enjoy my videos and blog posts. Thanks for the support! :)

Chloe.Claire1: Oh goodness, I'm so sorry! I had no idea you also wrote blog posts too! I'll be sure to read through all of them right now, and subscribe so as not to miss out on any future articles you write. I'm sure you write with as much elegance and eloquence as you speak with in your videos.

FilmFanFaye: Haha there's certainly no pressure. But if you like my writing, feel free to let me know and share it around! :)

——— ··•·· ———

Chloe.Claire1: Oh Faye, you really do write with as much elegance as you speak with, just as I suspected you would. Perhaps even moreso! I have already learned so much from your articles and videos about the world of cinema and I am excited—positively vibrating—to learn even more from you in the future. I do hope you have a long and lucrative career as a film critic. You have such a wonderful eye for great stories.

FilmFanFaye: Aw thanks, Chloe! I'm really touched. You're sweet. It's a difficult industry to get into, which is why I made my own channel and blog. I'd like to be able to monetise those by myself because freelancing is a constant battle. Support from lovely people like you really means a lot, though, thank you! :)

Chloe.Claire1: I am so deeply sorry to hear that freelancing is hard and that the industry is tough. Your words are beautiful and your knowledge is deep; you deserve to have your words reach far and wide. As I said, I have already learned so much from you in this short yet wonderful time! I was forbidden from watching movies as a child, and now that I'm grown up I feel so far behind. There is an entire world of cinema (not to mention books and music and so much more) for me to explore! I only wish to have time enough for it all!

FilmFanFaye: I'm sorry you had such a rough childhood, Chloe :(Mine wasn't always easy either. And I actually didn't find a passion for cinema until I was at university, so there's always time. Like you said, it's a wide world, and exploring it will be very exciting for you :)

Chloe.Claire1: Ah Faye, you have so effortlessly lifted my spirits yet again. You're wonderful at doing that and I am immensely grateful every single time you do so. Perhaps there is hope for me after all! As a child, my mother owned a TV but wouldn't let me near it, and family trips simply never happened, let alone to the cinema to see the latest blockbusters. I have only discovered that vast world of cinema fairly recently and what a wonderful journey it has turned out to be! My mother has very little power over me these days, and so I am almost free to lose myself in movies to my heart's content.

FilmFanFaye: Wow, sorry you had such a controlling mother growing up, Chloe. Well done for escaping all that and finding your own hobbies and interests.

Chloe.Claire1: Thank you so much, dear Faye. Unfortunately, I am not entirely free of her as I must still share a roof with her for the time being. But she is far more lenient with me these days, and I have a space of my own in which to watch good movies and read good books. And now I also have you, shining like a torch to guide me in the right direction as I venture out into this new world of visual arts.

FilmFanFaye: I'm glad to hear that. Having your own space is important :)

Chloe.Claire1 liked that.

----- ..•.. -----

Comment from @Chloe.Claire1:
Goodness me, what a wonderful analysis of this film. You certainly seem to have managed to pull back the layers of surrealism to expose the beating heart underneath. And what a heart it is! I struggle so much with surrealism myself, because I often take things at face value. I did not learn the skills to dig deeper, and so I hope to be able to learn some of those skills from you, dear Faye. I will endeavour to think more critically in the future when watching new movies.

Reply from @FilmFanFaye:
Practice makes perfect when it comes to analysis, just like anything else. And I'm not saying that my interpretation is the right one, or even a good one. But I have fun doing it. I'm sure you can, too :)

Reply from @Chloe.Claire1:
Oh Faye, thank you for having such faith in me. I am not used to someone believing in me the way that you do. I hope that I will not let you down. I want to be able to do what you do, and show you all that I have learned from you. Perhaps you are right (in fact, I'm sure you are) and I can learn to see the beauty and the hidden parts of stories in the same way that you do. You make it seem so effortless, but I will dedicate myself to the craft as best I can. Please believe in me.

----- ..•.. -----

Chloe.Claire1: Dearest Faye, thank you for what you said in the comments of your latest video. Having someone who believes in me is a wonderful thing. Last night, I endeavoured to watch a horror movie (the same one that you spoke so highly about recently) and see what themes I could glean from its text and visual presentation. Unfortunately—and I hope you won't be angry with or disappointed in me—I was left feeling so afraid that I could glean little from the movie at all. It left me in a state of fright and paralysis that didn't let me go for some time. I had such horrible nightmares as a result. But I will try again with something more friendly tonight. Thank you, dear Faye, for having faith in me.

FilmFanFaye: Please don't watch anything that might frighten or upset you, Chloe! I hate the idea that my recommendations are causing anyone harm. My videos are just vehicles for me to express my thoughts about the things I enjoy, that's all. If a film is going to scare you, don't watch it.

Chloe.Claire1: Oh Faye, I do hope you are not angry with me for what I did. I only wished to act on the inspiration you have instilled in me. Please do not be angry with me. I have spent so much of my life making people upset, and so often I do not know what I have done wrong. This time, I think I do understand how I have upset you and I will do what I can to not disappoint you again. Please believe me.

FilmFanFaye: I'm not angry with you at all, Chloe! I'm only worried about you. I don't want anyone getting nightmares off my recommendations. Like I said before, please take care of yourself :)

Chloe.Claire1: My heart soars with the relief that you are not upset or disappointed. I do so fear upsetting you, even more than I fear the things I saw in that horror movie. You are so kind and patient with me, dear Faye. Thank you. I will let you know what beautiful things I see in the next movie I watch.

FilmFanFaye: That sounds great, please do! :)

Chloe.Claire1 liked that.

Comment from @Chloe.Claire1:
This movie sounds so incredibly moving and wholesome! Just the thing that so many people, myself included, need right now. I have had a few difficult days, both personally and professionally, and a movie like this one is just the thing I need to lift my spirits and give me hope for a brighter future. May it clear away the clouds and reveal a brighter sky.

Reply from @FilmFanFaye:
Sorry you've been having a tough time but I hope the film gives you the good vibes you deserve :)

Reply from @Chloe.Claire1:
Thank you as always, dear Faye, for your kind and considerate response. My mother has been returning to her old frightening ways lately. She is so horribly unpredictable and I often wonder if I am safe under her roof, though I have very little choice at the moment and so I must soldier on. You give me the strength I need, and the means of escaping this frightening

time through the magic of cinema. Thank you, as always, kind heart.

———··•··———

Chloe.Claire1: My dearest Faye, I must offer you my warmest congratulations! I saw your latest post about hitting such an enormous milestone in your subscriber count! What an incredible feat. I am so glad you are getting the attention and recognition you deserve, though I am also not surprised. You are so brilliantly talented, after all!

———··•··———

Chloe.Claire1: Lovely Faye, I hope I did not offend you in any way with my previous message? Perhaps my saying that I was not surprised was tinged with too much arrogance. Sometimes I struggle with saying the right things and I would never want to offend you. I hope you are not ignoring me as a means of punishing me.

FilmFanFaye: Sorry, Chloe, I've just been busy with work recently. And I was inundated with lots of lovely messages of congratulations, yours included! I'm so grateful for your continued support and I'm humbled by how much the channel has grown so quickly. It's very exciting :)

Chloe.Claire1: Oh this comes as such relief! I was desperately afraid that I had upset you and caused you to shut me out. It is a tactic I am very familiar with. My mother would often do the same to me for days, even weeks at a time. I am glad to have not upset you in the same way.

FilmFanFaye: I'm so sorry that you had to deal with such abusive treatment from your mum when you were a kid, Chloe. Nobody deserves that, and you're obviously a very good and kind person. Like I said, I was just busy and that's why I didn't respond.

Chloe.Claire1: Thank you for your kind words and your understanding, dear Faye. You always show me such care and compassion. I should have trusted you not to shut me out. I know you far better than that, and I'm sure that if I were to upset you in any way, you would tell me honestly.

Comment from @Chloe.Claire1:
Another wonderful list! I'm sure that your fans and followers appreciate all the attention you are giving to smaller indie projects like these ones. You are opening our eyes to so many magical movies that very often get overlooked, which is such a shame. You work so hard, and your videos continue to be a light in the darkness for me when life proves difficult.

Reply from @FilmFanFaye:
Thank you, Chloe :)

Comment from @Chloe.Claire1:
Oh! This video touched me so deeply! I can't imagine the courage it must take to open yourself up like this in front of a camera and discuss your personal life so candidly. I am very proud and appreciative, as are so many other people, I'm sure.

Discussing your feelings and struggles in this way will undoubtedly help other people, and encourage them to do the same in turn.

Reply from @FilmFanFaye:
Glad you enjoyed the video :) Being open and honest in front of an audience isn't an easy thing to do but, like I said in the video, I hope I can bring some hope and comfort to other trans and non-binary people :)

Reply from @Chloe.Claire1:
I completely agree. When we share our own stories, we let people know that they are not alone with their fears and anxieties. I feel alone so terribly often, and having your channel to keep me company on the quietest of days brings me so much solace and warmth. Thank you, Faye, always and forever. You are beautiful.

Chloe.Claire1: Dearest Faye, I truly meant every word I said in my comments on your latest video. Posting a personal video all about your own life must take such an enormous amount of courage. I fear I would never be able to do the same thing, but once again you have inspired me.

FilmFanFaye: That's sweet of you to say, Chloe, thank you. Being an openly trans person on the Internet is never fun, even if you keep to yourself. And since my platform is growing, I felt like using it to try and do some good. Maybe I can inspire other people to speak up, feel proud, or just feel less alone :)

Chloe.Claire1: You have certainly done just that. You must have younger followers who are questioning their gender identities, and seeing you go through good days and bad days along your own gender journey is going to make them feel much less alone. I myself have been questioning my own gender identity for some time now, and so your video spoke to me in truly profound ways. While I cannot open up to my mother (or anyone in my family for that matter) about my feelings concerning gender expression, I hope that I can confide in you. I feel that you will understand what I am going through more than anyone.

FilmFanFaye: Everyone's life experience is unique, but I can always lend you an ear if you need someone to talk to :)

Chloe.Claire1: Oh thank you, dear Faye, thank you! I never knew my father; my sister left home several years ago; and my mother, as you know, is a very unsympathetic, often cruel woman. Having to hide who I am has grown from an emotional pain into an almost physical one. Not being able to express my true gender identity is like having multiple thorns in my skin that I cannot pull free.

FilmFanFaye: What have you come to realise about yourself?

Chloe.Claire1: Thank you so much for asking. I believe that the best term to fit how I feel is "non-binary". I know, from reading your older blog posts, that this is how you identified before coming out as a transgender woman, and I feel that it is a definition that fits me comfortably. I was born a woman, you see, but sometimes that word feels as though it itches. I do not like or trust men at all, and do not feel a kinship with manhood. And yet femininity hardly feels comfortable for me either.

FilmFanFaye: I relate to a lot of what you're saying, Chloe. I don't have much trust in men either, and masculinity has always made me feel uncomfortable. For me, femininity feels like a home. For you, your home might be outside of the gender binary entirely, and that's wonderful. I'm happy for you :)

Chloe.Claire1: Oh my wonderful Faye, I knew you would understand! Yes, that is it exactly! I do not feel as though I am either a man or a woman. I simply wish to be me. Perhaps I should start going by they/them pronouns?

FilmFanFaye: That's totally your call to make, Chloe. Nobody can tell you what will fit you best. Try it on for size and see. As someone who, like you said, identified as non-binary for a time, I'm still very connected to the non-binary experience and still wish we could do away with the binary altogether! But at the same time, I know that being a woman makes me happy :)

Chloe.Claire1: And you are such a beautiful woman, Faye! Inside and out! I think I shall try using they/them pronouns and see how they suit me. Removing myself from the binary feels like an exciting and liberating thing to do. I know that my mother will not understand, and will likely reject me for it but I must hold my head high and still try my very best to be who I am, to be my true and authentic self. If I feel lost or frightened along my own gender journey, I can remember your words and think about how far you've come. I'll be inspired by you and your courage, dear Faye. I have called you my light in the darkness more than once before, and it remains true. Perhaps now more than ever before.

FilmFanFaye: I'm very glad I could help. Let me know how the pronouns suit you :)

Chloe.Claire1 liked that.

Chloe.Claire1: Oh Faye, I saw some of the comments you've been receiving recently since coming out and discussing your transition. I am so sorry for the cruelty the world can sometimes throw at people like us. My own mother has been especially cruel to me for the past few days after I asked her to respect my pronouns and my new gender identity. She even threatened to lock me out of the house, knowing that I would have nowhere to go.

FilmFanFaye: I'm really sorry to hear that, Chloe. Didn't you mention a sister before? Could you not go and stay with her?

Chloe.Claire1: Unfortunately, she is no less cruel than our mother is. Growing up, she internalised so much of what our mother taught her and has very much grown, over time, into a copy of our mother. She has children of her own now, as well, and would not appreciate me taking up space in her home. There would not be room for me. Fortunately, my mother's words were an empty threat (for now, at least), and I do still have my home. I hope that my mother will see reason and come to treat me with a little more love and respect.

FilmFanFaye: I don't know you or your mother, Chloe, but if you're an adult who lived through a rough childhood, I wouldn't hold out much hope for your mother to change now. Might it not be better for you to think about moving out and getting free of this toxic situation?

Chloe.Claire1: You are quite right, my dear Faye. That would be the best move for me to make. Unfortunately, I am not currently in a strong enough financial situation to do so. My job is only part-time and does not pay enough for me to find my own place to live right now.

FilmFanFaye: I'm so sorry to hear that, Chloe. I've also struggled for money for the past few years so I do empathise. I guess just keep an eye open for a new job and do your best to save so that you can get out of there and live your best life :)

Chloe.Claire1: Thank you, Faye. I do so dream of the day when I can turn my back on my mother and rid myself of her once and for all. She will not have control over me and my life forever. She cannot. I will continue to be inspired by the things you say and do, and work to be a free person as soon as possible. Thank you, as always, for your kind words of inspiration and motivation.

———··●··———

Chloe.Claire1: Dearest Faye, today my mother screamed at me in the supermarket. We were shopping for groceries and the cashier called me "miss". I explained that I use they/them pronouns and my mother laughed at me loudly. When I tried to explain myself to her, she got angry very quickly (she has often done this—switching from mockery to anger in a moment). She shouted at me in front of the cashier and I was so frightened that I felt as though I might wet myself! But I didn't; I gritted my teeth and stood firm, thinking about how strong you are in the face of online abuse. Thank you for continuing to inspire and comfort me, Faye.

FilmFanFaye: Chloe, online abuse and domestic abuse are very different things. I can block the trolls and shut my laptop, but you are in a much more vulnerable position. Are you not able to call the police?

Chloe.Claire1: You are right, dear Faye, they are different. Sadly, I doubt the police would help me, given how I am an adult and my mother takes care not to physically injure me. She shouts and threatens and mocks me, but that is not enough for anyone to step in and protect me. Oh, Faye, I feel so dreadfully alone and helpless at times like these. Thank you for always listening to me and giving me advice. You are a true and kind friend to me.

FilmFanFaye: Please look after yourself, Chloe, and go somewhere safe if you can.

Comment from @Chloe.Claire1:

I saw this movie myself recently, and it reminded me of the bond my sister and I once shared as children. Like the protagonist, I grew up in a small village and had only my sister to play with. We were very close, having tea parties inside and playing make-believe in the forest behind our home. It was a magical time, where the world was just us and nobody else. Nothing to hurt us or distract us from each other. But we all grow up and grow apart eventually. While I didn't lose my sister like the protagonist of this film did, I have certainly lost the bond we once shared. She is no longer my sister, not as she once was, not as I once considered her to be. It is a sad thing, to grow and change. I am glad you enjoyed this movie, as even though it triggered a mix of happy and sad memories in me, I also appreciate its beauty.

Reply from @FilmFanFaye:
I'm sorry you and your sister have grown apart, but at least you have those memories to look back on, and it's nice to have a piece of art that speaks to you in such an intimate way :)

Reply from @Chloe.Claire1:
Oh Faye, you are very right as always. I'm sure I will watch this film again in the months and years to come, and enjoy flashes of my own childhood memories with my sister as I do so. Back then, our mother was like a force of nature, belittling and frightening and sometimes hurting us. But we always had each other, until we didn't anymore, and my sister began acting much like our mother had. I fear for her children—my niece and nephews—but there is little I can do in my current situation. And so I will hold onto this film and the memories it churns up for me. You have a wonderful heart, dear Faye, thank you.

Chloe.Claire1: It happened again, Faye. My mother and I were out together running some errands (we visited the post office, the bookshop, and gave some old things to charity). I mentioned to her the memories of my sister that the film had conjured, and my mother grew impatient and snapped at me. She told me that she hated those years when we were young, that we were difficult children to raise, that we were selfish and petulant girls. I told her that I'm not a girl, and that she was cruel to us as children. She abused us terribly. This made her red with rage, and she turned to me in the middle of the street with an angry scowl and a raised hand. I knew she wanted to hit me, and she came so close, dear Faye, but remembering that she was in public, in broad daylight, caused her to stop just before she laid a finger on me. We are back home now, and she is currently busying herself with a few chores, but I fear what she will do if I anger her again, especially while we are alone together in the house.

FilmFanFaye: Is there nowhere safe you can go? And if she does try to hurt you, you can always call the police.

Chloe.Claire1: Your concern means so much to me, lovely Faye, thank you. Unfortunately, there is nowhere for me to go. I don't drive and we live in a small town. My sister lives far away and I have no friends or family within reach. Even if I did, I fear being a nuisance and causing them any kind of disruption.

FilmFanFaye: You wouldn't be a nuisance, Chloe. People are very understanding when someone needs a safe place.

Chloe.Claire1: Thank you, Faye, though I believe you to be one-of-a-kind. While you show me a wonderful amount of understanding and kindness, what little family I still have would never be so considerate. I can only hope that my mother calms herself down, and that I can avoid saying or doing anything that might upset her or cause her to spiral into a fit of anger.

Chloe.Claire1: Dearest Faye, I went to bed early last night in the hopes of protecting myself from my mother, but just as she often did when I was a child, she drank herself into a stupor and woke me up in the dark of night to frighten and threaten and spit at me. She said such dreadful things to me, Faye. She slammed her clenched fists into my bedding, and I know that of course she wanted to throw them at me but she held back, thankfully. She told me that she regretted having me and my sister, that I was a millstone around her neck, and that I remain one now. I am so afraid, Faye. She is growing worse, back to how she was when I was small, and she hurt me back then so I'm sure she will hit me again soon.

FilmFanFaye: That is so dreadful, Chloe, I'm sorry. If she does hurt you, you must call the police for protection. And, if she dislikes having you in her home, it's all the more reason for you to find somewhere else to live.

Chloe.Claire1: You are so kind and caring, lovely Faye, and you are right. I know that you are. Sadly, for all she says (and so often shouts) about me being a burden and a waste, she wants me to stay with her. She keeps a roof over my head and charges me nothing for it. She always takes me with her when she goes shopping; she won't leave without me, in fact. I don't have the financial means to leave, and even if I did, I fear that she would be lost without me.

FilmFanFaye: Finances aside, it doesn't seem like she has earned your sympathy. You sound like you're worried about her, which I guess is kind of you, but you need to protect yourself. You are living with an abuser, Chloe, and you need to get to safety. Let me see if there are any charities that might give support to someone in your position.

Chloe.Claire1: My dear Faye, I have never known anyone take such care of me before, not like you do. You give me so much love and compassion. I wish I could do more for you in return but, sadly, I am not worth much.

FilmFanFaye: Everyone's worth the same amount, Chloe. That's just your mother talking. Here, I've sent you a link to a domestic abuse charity. Please consider giving them a call.

Chloe.Claire1: Beautiful Faye, thank you for taking the time to find me some help. I know that I cannot repay you, and show you all the love that you so deserve, but I do so appreciate your kindness and your consideration. You have a beautiful soul, and I don't think I would be here without the light it provides me. You illuminate my life, my glowing Faye.

———··•··———

Comment from @Chloe.Claire1: While I don't think I could watch a movie like this one in my current fragile state, I did recently re-watch one of the few films I was allowed to sit through as a child. My sister and I saw it more than once; in fact, we would sometimes sit in front of the TV for entire afternoons watching, rewinding, and re-watching it again three or four times. The movie showed me such warmth and sparked my imagination as a child. This time, it reminded me so vividly of all those feelings, but it also threw into sharp relief the situation in which I currently find myself: one of danger and insecurity and trepidation. I am not safe, and thinking back to those brief moments where I did feel safe as a child only served to highlight my present dangers. What I thought would be a happy viewing experience became a sickly reminder of just how threatened and unwanted I currently feel. The ways in which the universe tells me over and again, each and every day, that I am worth so little. Nothing at all, in fact. Nothing at all.

Reply from FilmFanFaye: We all feel worthless from time to time. These feelings pass. It's a good idea to lose yourself in films at times like these, but I guess we just have to choose those films carefully. Escape into something safe and happy, Chloe, and remember that you are worth so much :)

Reply from @Chloe.Claire1: Oh Faye, kind and sweet Faye, your dedication to my wellbeing is something I often curse myself for taking for granted. It is so loud and clear, as is your good heart. I will not squander the kindness you show me, and I will tell myself that I am not worthless, that my mother is a liar, that my sister is useless, that I am better than them, and that I am loved. I am loved.

Chloe.Claire1: Beautiful Faye, did you mean what you said in your reply to my comment today, about how I am loved?

FilmFanFaye: We are all loved and appreciated, Chloe. Everyone has the capacity for love, and we show each other kindness and compassion each and every day, even just through good manners and a smile.

Chloe.Claire1: Oh and my dear, lovely Faye, you do show me this kind of love and compassion every single day. Your words set my soul ablaze. I likely would not be here without you. In fact, I know that I would not. You have given me so much courage. When my mother plunges me into darkness, there is always a light left on, and you are that light. Thank you. I love you so dearly.

FilmFanFaye: Chloe, you don't need me to teach you courage. You're an adult with plenty of your own strength. You have all the knowledge and resources you need to keep yourself safe, and to get out of this difficult situation on your own. I know you can do it.

Chloe.Claire1: Thank you for believing in me, dearest Faye, even when I don't and can't believe in myself. I will make you proud. I will get myself out of this situation. I will be free of my mother's clutches, and it will be thanks to the kindness and courage you have provided me.

FilmFanFaye: Once again, your courage is your own. Just call the police if your mother hurts you, and get in contact with the charity I linked you to, okay?

Chloe.Claire1 liked that.

Chloe.Claire1: My sweet Faye, I have done a terrible thing. Although, truthfully, I do not feel guilty about it at all. In fact, I feel freed by my choices and my actions. I am not sure what to do next or where to go, but I am glad to have finally made a choice of my own for the first time in my life.

FilmFanFaye: What do you mean? What have you done?

Chloe.Claire1: I have killed my mother, dear Faye. I cut and stabbed her several times, before plunging the knife deep into her wretched heart. The heart she never used. A dark and empty heart that is no longer beating, that didn't ever deserve to beat. I thought carefully about what you said, about how I have courage and that I am loved, that you love me, dear Faye. I used that courage to kill her, to stop her, to shut her up forever, to keep her from ever hurting me again. Thanks to you, I know what real love looks and feels like. My mother never showed me love, only pain and spite and cruelty, and so I have killed her, and now I can be free of her. All that's left is a vacant body and some blood, which can be washed away.

FilmFanFaye: Chloe, I'm calling the police. What's your address?

Chloe.Claire1: You don't need to do that, my dear Faye. I told you that I have killed her myself, with my own hands. You don't need to call the police. She is dead. I am free.

Chloe.Claire1: Oh my dear Faye, I heard the terrible sirens before I saw them. A neighbour must have heard the screams. But don't worry; I soon realised how the scene would look to them, and that I would be blamed, even though I was only performing justice and freeing myself from her tyranny. I have managed to escape out the back and through the garden. I am out and free for now. I don't know where I can go but I will make my own way. I have the courage you lent me. Thank you, my lovely Faye, for all that you have done to help me. I love you so dearly.

Chloe.Claire1: I do not have much money available to me, dear Faye, but I have managed to get myself to London. I rode the bus, and it took a while, but I am here now. It is busy and there are so many people, but I have your courage. I know that you live here in London; you have mentioned it before in your videos. Please, come and find me. I want to feel your love and your warmth in person, for myself, just for me. I will walk the streets of London until I find you, and then I will be able to return the love that you have shown me, my dearest Faye.

A MOTHER'S LOVE

WRITTEN BY WILLOW HEATH
DIRECTED BY DAVID JONES

Scene 1

The majority of the stage remains dark. A single sickly yellow spotlight illuminates Cassandra, stage right. She is wearing a buttoned-up brown coat, black leggings, and black Chelsea boots. She is standing still, legs pressed together, head bowed, one arm crossing her middle. She is speaking on her mobile phone.

CASSANDRA: Yes, mum, I know. I know. I've been busy. I'm sorry.

Long pause.

Cassandra sighs.

CASSANDRA: I know, yes, I said I was sorry. I'll come visit you this weekend, all right?

Pause.

CASSANDRA: I've just been busy, that's all. Work, personal stuff. Well, I can tell you this weekend, can't I?

Pause.

[Director's note: Cassandra needs to speak more quickly, but also quietly. There should be a quaver in her voice. We'll work on that at the next vocal training session.]

CASSANDRA: Right, yes, see you then. I don't know what time exactly. I'll be there as early as possible. We can have the whole weekend together.

Pause.

CASSANDRA: Love you, too.

Cassandra sharply removes her phone from her ear, sniffs, and drops it into her tote bag. She rubs the skin beneath her eyes with her little fingers, sniffs again, tucks her hair behind both ears, lifts her head, clears her throat, and exits stage right. The light dims.

Scene 2

Soft lighting illuminates the stage. A bookcase lined with books stands stage left, and another filled with knick-knacks, ornaments, and framed photographs stands stage right. A two-seater sofa sits in the centre; a low coffee table in front of it. On the sofa is a half-filled open suitcase.

Cassandra enters stage right, carrying a bundle of folded knitwear in her arms. She drops it into the open suitcase and proceeds to silently rearrange the other items and clothing. She removes a black skirt and holds it up at arm's length for a moment, before replacing it in the suitcase.

Mary, wearing a yellow set of pyjama shirt and trousers, enters stage left, cradling a bowl of crisps in one arm. She takes and eats one. She stands behind the sofa, watching Cassandra pack.

MARY: Are you sure you need that much stuff? How long are you going for?

CASSANDRA: Three nights.

MARY: What about work? Are you taking Monday off?

CASSANDRA: Just the morning. I'll leave early and be at the office by lunchtime.

Cassandra exists stage right.

MARY: Still seems a bit much for three nights.

CASSANDRA (offstage): This suitcase is all I've got. Unless

you have a holdall or a hiking bag I can borrow?

Cassandra returns, carrying a toiletry bag in one hand.

MARY: No, sorry.

CASSANDRA: Then it'll have to do, won't it. I'm not actually taking much. It just looks like a lot.

MARY: And you're going to be okay?

Mary takes and eats another crisp before setting the bowl down on the coffee table.

[Director's note: Mary's clothing should be more open and relaxed. Pyjama shorts instead of trousers. Switch from yellow to red. And her hair shouldn't be tied up in a messy bun. Maybe let it flow down her back? We'll play around with it at the next rehearsal.]

CASSANDRA: Probably not, but I've said I'll go. It's only two full days. There's not much she can do to me in that time.

MARY: And you're going to tell her?

CASSANDRA: Well, I can't exactly hide it, can I?

MARY: She'll see what she wants to see.

CASSANDRA: Right, but I also don't want to hide it. Not anymore. It's just me.

Cassandra zips up the suitcase and places both hands on top of it. Mary crosses the stage and hugs Cassandra from behind, kissing her shoulder and the top of her head.

MARY: You come home any time you want to. Or call me and I'll come running. You sure you don't want me there? I'm still happy to come; I can take the time off work. It's no problem at all.

CASSANDRA: No, I hate dragging you into family stuff. I can do this by myself. And I kind of feel like I should. But you're right, I'll leave if it gets too much. Or if she kicks me out.

MARY: I doubt she'd do that.

Cassandra silently lifts the suitcase and carries it to the edge of the stage, then exits stage left. The lights slowly go down on Mary as she picks up the bowl and eats another crisp.

[Director's note: Cassandra needs to struggle more when she lifts the suitcase.]

Scene 3

A pair of lamps—one standing stage right, the other on a table centrestage—illuminate most of the stage, with the area stage left slightly obscured in shadow. Twin armchairs sit either side of the centre table and lamp. The armchairs each have a frayed, faded patchwork blanket draped neatly over them.

Diane enters from stage left. She is wearing a thick beige dressing gown and woolly slippers, decorated to look like a pair of sheep. Under her arm is a newspaper, which she unfolds and begins to read as she sits in the nearest armchair to her.

A knocking sound offstage.

CASSANDRA (offstage): Hi mum, it's me.

Diane grunts, gets to her feet, crosses the stage, and opens the door stage right, then steps back. Cassandra takes one step onto the stage and leans in to hug her mother with one arm, keeping the other hand on her suitcase handle. Diane returns the hug without a word.

Diane crosses the stage and returns to her armchair, gesturing to the other one with a polite smile. Cassandra removes her coat and drapes it over her suitcase, then tucks her suitcase behind the empty armchair before sitting down opposite her mother.

DIANE: You look well, love. Mary's cooking must agree with you.

CASSANDRA: We mostly cook together but, yes, they're her

recipes, and they're all so delicious.

DIANE: That's good, that's good. And she's well, is she?

CASSANDRA: Very well, yeah.

DIANE: And work?

CASSANDRA: Work's good. I leave a little later than I'd like to at the moment because they've piled on a few extra responsibilities, but it's fine.

DIANE: That sounds like a good thing to me.

CASSANDRA: Well, it's because of poor management, really. They let someone go recently, and then they split his work up amongst three other people, and I'm one of them.

DIANE: I'd still take it as a compliment. And there's nothing wrong with a bit of extra work, is there.

CASSANDRA: We aren't getting paid for it, though.

Diane sighs through her nose and clears her throat.

DIANE: Tea?

CASSANDRA: Why don't I make it?

Cassandra crosses the stage in front of Diane and exits stage left.

Diane looks at the floor for a moment, then clears her throat.

DIANE: They let you wear that to work, do they?

CASSANDRA (offstage): What do you mean?

DIANE: That skirt.

CASSANDRA (offstage): It's part of the dress code. I'm not breaking any rules.

DIANE: I beg to differ.

CASSANDRA (offstage): What does that mean?

DIANE: Well, it's hardly appropriate is it, Derek, love?

CASSANDRA (offstage): Please don't call me that.

DIANE: What?

Silence. The sound of cutlery knocking against china can be heard offstage.

DIANE: Please be careful with the china!

Cassandra reenters holding two steaming mugs of tea. She sets one down on the table next to her mother and cradles the other as she sits back down in her armchair.

DIANE: Your brother has told me about these things you're doing.

CASSANDRA: What things?

Diane gestures to Cassandra's hair and clothing.

DIANE: All of this. Growing your hair out and wearing skirts. You're a little old to be going through a phase like this, Derek, don't you think?

CASSANDRA: It's not a phase, mum. That's what I wanted to talk to you about.

[Director's note: Cassandra should be holding back tears here. Maybe a catch in ~~his~~ her throat and a nervous twitch or something. We'll get him to tap ~~his~~ her foot.]

DIANE: Right, go on, then.

Diane sits up straight and slowly sips at her tea. She looks across to Cassandra, expectantly.

CASSANDRA: I know that you've noticed all the changes that have been going on with me, mum. You've already made a few comments, and that makes this as hard for me to talk about as it is for you to hear. But this is something that I've been exploring for a while. I've come to know and understand myself better. And love myself better, too. I've talked to a psychiatrist… not that I should have to, but I followed all the rules. I'm making the necessary legal changes on all my paperwork. I've told everyone at work, and they've been pretty supportive and accommodating, all things considered. The only person left to talk to is you, and I'm sure you can understand why I saved you for last.

Cassandra takes a slow, deep breath in and out.

I'm a woman, mum. And my name is Cassandra.

Cassandra smiles to herself and breathes a light sigh. Her shoulders relax.

DIANE: Right.

Diane maintains eye contact and pulls an exaggerated frown. She sips her tea again.

DIANE: And how does Mary feel about all this? She can't have taken it very well, having her boyfriend trying on her clothes.

A pause. Cassandra stares at her mug and takes a few quiet breaths.

CASSANDRA: She's fine. She's known for a long time. Nothing's changed between us. We love each other just the same. In fact, things are even better now, I think, because I'm happier. She loves that I'm happy.

DIANE: Your brother told me something about it.

CASSANDRA: Yes, I assumed as much.

DIANE: He's very confused about the whole thing.

CASSANDRA: I'm not sure that's true, is it, mum? Chris and I talk all the time. He's been lovely about it from the start, as I knew he would be. My brother's a good guy; always has been. He started calling me his sister from day one. Said he's happy to have a sister, actually.

DIANE: And when was this day one? How long has he known?

CASSANDRA: A while. A few months, maybe.

DIANE: And you're just telling me about this now?

CASSANDRA: I already told you that it should be obvious why I saved you for last. This—this behaviour right here—this is why finding the strength to talk to you about it has been hard. And anyway, it's really not about you, mum. If I thought this conversation was going to be easy, we could have had it a long time ago. I would have been proud to tell you before anyone else, but it could never have played out that way.

DIANE: So you put it off because you thought I'd be difficult?

CASSANDRA: You *are* being difficult. If you already knew from Chris then you wouldn't have belittled me by calling it a phase.

DIANE: You never stopped to consider my feelings about all of this? I am still your mother, you know.

From the darkened corner behind Diane, a figure steps forward: a pale, naked man with a potbelly. His face is obscured by a mask. The mask is of a blank human expression.

Cassandra jumps to her feet and points.

CASSANDRA: What the hell is that?

Diane turns around, frowning and snorting.

DIANE: What's what? There's nothing there, love. Did you see a mouse or something?

CASSANDRA: Mum, there's a man! Standing right behind you. He's naked.

Diane turns back to Cassandra and chuckles.

DIANE: Really, Derek, first the skirts and now this? What's gotten into you? You're acting like a petulant child.

The naked figure retreats into the darkness.

CASSANDRA: There was a man, mum. Wearing a mask.

DIANE (laughing): Well, how do you know he was a man? Might have been a woman behind that mask. You're suddenly a woman and you've still got a penis. Oh, God, you're not going to get that hideous operation, are you?

CASSANDRA: Mum! He was standing right behind you.

[Director's note: This line should be delivered with a shriller voice. It's far too deep right now. We'll have to practise that.]

DIANE: Really, Derek. Well where is he now? Or she?

CASSANDRA: Stop it.

DIANE: Or they. That's a thing now as well, isn't it? You can be a they now. Two people. I always thought that was called a split personality.

Diane chuckles to herself.

CASSANDRA: You can't make me leave. I'm going to bed and we're spending the weekend together, just like you wanted.

DIANE: Who said anything about leaving?

CASSANDRA: What makes you think this is a nice environment for me to be in? I have no reason to stay. But I'm going to. I'll stay for the whole weekend, and if you still won't accept me and call me by my name by Monday morning, then you won't be seeing me again.

DIANE: I have been calling you by your name. The one your father and I gave you. God knows what he'd think of all this, rest his soul.

CASSANDRA: That's not my name, mum. I'm grateful for it but I've chosen my own now, and it fits me better.

Silence. Cassandra crosses the stage in front of Diane and exits stage left. The lights fade on Diane.

Scene 4

A faint glow of moonlight illuminates the stage. In one armchair sits the naked masked man. Enter Cassandra stage left, wearing pyjamas, her hair tied back in a ponytail. She crosses half the stage before noticing the man, reclining in the chair, his knees spread wide apart. She screams.

CASSANDRA: What the fuck are you doing in here? Get out!

She steps backwards, clutching one clasped hand to her chest and pointing offstage with the other. The man grabs his flaccid penis and starts to rub it until it stiffens.

CASSANDRA: Is this a joke? Get the fuck out!

The man scratches at his chest and neck with his free hand while continuing to masturbate with the other.

CASSANDRA: Get out right now or I'll throw you out.

Cassandra steps towards the man. He quickly gets to his feet and towers over her, his erect penis pointing directly at her. She stops and shuffles backwards. The man replaces his hand and continues to tug on his penis. He steps towards her, and she steps back, keeping the same distance between them. Cassandra, her lip quivering, pauses for a moment before turning and fleeing stage left. The stage darkens.

[Director's note: Replace the actor playing the man. Someone less fat and hairy. Also, Cassandra should shrink more when he stands up. Make her look smaller.]

Scene 5

The lights come up on Cassandra and Diane sitting in the living room, each with a plate of toast on her lap and a mug of coffee next to her.

DIANE: So, why Cassandra?

CASSANDRA: Are you coming around to it?

DIANE: I'm simply curious.

CASSANDRA: It just came to me. When I looked in the mirror and saw what I really was, Cassandra was just there, honestly. It felt like she had been waiting for me.

DIANE: Oh, for heaven's sake, Derek. What you really are, love, is a boy. I saw that the moment you were born.

CASSANDRA: I wasn't born a marketing manager either, mum, and yet I am one.

Diane crunches her toast and takes a sip of her coffee.

CASSANDRA: I saw that man again last night.

DIANE: What man?

CASSANDRA: The one in the mask. I came downstairs for a wee and he was in here, wanking.

DIANE: I beg your pardon!

CASSANDRA: Last night, in the dark, there was a man in this room having a wank.

DIANE: Oh Derek, if you're going to be this vulgar please just leave. I can't be dealing with you like this.

CASSANDRA: Like what? I saw a fat naked man sitting in your chair—

DIANE: —That's enough, Derek!

CASSANDRA: My name is Cassandra.

DIANE: Oh for God's sake, no it isn't. It says Derek on your birth certificate. I know. I chose it. I was there.

CASSANDRA: Well, it says Cassandra on my driver's licence and my debit card and my passport—

DIANE: —Oh you really have taken this too far, now.

Diane gets up with her empty plate and exits stage left.

A moment later, the masked man enters through the same doorway, stage left. He steps towards Cassandra. His shoulders shrug up and down as though he is laughing. Cassandra stands up.

CASSANDRA: For fuck's sake. Mum, he's here again!

The naked man closes the gap between himself and Cassandra, his flaccid penis gently swinging between his legs.

CASSANDRA: Don't come near me. Mum! Where are you?

Cassandra raises her fist to threaten him, but the man continues towards her. She throws her fist at him but he swats it away and takes her by the throat with one hand. With the other hand he squeezes his penis for a moment, then touches her chest. His shoulders bob up and down again.

CASSANDRA (struggling): Get the fuck off me.

She kicks him in the shins, and clumsily slaps him in the side of his head. The clattering of plates and cutlery can be heard offstage. The man releases Cassandra and retreats stage left.

[Director's note: Before she kicks him, Cassandra should whimper and cry. I want to hear some struggling noises.]

Diane re-enters stage left.

CASSANDRA: Did you not fucking hear me?

DIANE: I heard something but I thought you were probably just yelling profanities at me or something.

CASSANDRA: Mum, he walked right past you. Into the kitchen. Did you not see him?

DIANE: Who?

CASSANDRA: Fuck's sake, the naked man. He attacked me! Look.

Cassandra shows Diane her neck. Diane waves her hand in front of her face.

DIANE: It does look a bit red but who could tell with all that makeup you're caking on these days? You look like a clown.

CASSANDRA: Women wear makeup, mum.

DIANE: Well, not all women. I don't. That's very sexist of you, Derek.

CASSANDRA: I came here to open up to you. To tell you that I'm a woman. That my girlfriend loves me. As does Chris. As do my friends. And to ask if you'll love and accept me, too.

DIANE: Love you? Yes. But how can I accept you, looking as silly as you do right now?

CASSANDRA: Then we're done.

Cassandra takes out her phone, taps the screen, then puts it to her ear.

CASSANDRA: Hey, you were right. Of course you were. Can you come get me? I know I could take the train but… no, yeah, thanks. See you soon. Love you, too.

DIANE: That was Mary, I take it? So, you're just leaving now. After you promised to spend the weekend with me.

CASSANDRA: This isn't a fun weekend for me, mum. And my love isn't unconditional. I deserve your respect and I don't have it.

DIANE: So that's it? Your girlfriend comes to get you and I just don't see you again?

CASSANDRA: You don't get to have it all, mum. You can't bully me and expect me to bend over and take it.

DIANE: Oh how vulgar, Derek! What in the world is wrong with you?

Cassandra strides quickly past her mother and exits stage left.

Scene 6

Cassandra enters stage left, carrying her suitcase. Diane is sat in the armchair stage right and the masked man stands, blocking the doorway stage right.

CASSANDRA: You can't keep me here.

DIANE: Clearly not. You're free to go, if that's what you want to do.

CASSANDRA: It's not what I want, mum, but it's what I need. For my own sanity. I have to look after myself.

DIANE: I always looked after you, Derek. And after your father died, it wasn't easy. But I did a good job as a parent. I know I did.

CASSANDRA: Yes you did, mum. Nobody is disagreeing with you. And I'm grateful. But now I'm asking you to simply call me your daughter and accept me for who I am.

DIANE: Who you *are* is my son, Derek.

CASSANDRA: Why is this so important to you? Why are you willing to hurt me in order to make yourself feel better? What does this accomplish?

DIANE: I'm not hurting you. You're the one who has hurt me. Coming in here dressed like that! Throwing away the name that your father and I gave you. Forcing everyone to call you a woman. It's embarrassing. Shameful!

The masked man folds his arms across his chest. His penis begins to thicken and rise.

CASSANDRA: None of this is about you or anyone else. I'm just doing what makes me happy. I'm being true to myself. And I'm not hurting anyone else in the process.

DIANE: That's not true, is it, Derek? You're hurting me. And you're hurting your father. You've taken the name we gave you and trodden all over it. Cassandra? What kind of name is that? It's ridiculous. You're a little boy playing dress-up. Do you want to try on my bra and knickers next?

CASSANDRA: Don't be disgusting, mum.

DIANE: Me? It's me who's disgusting, is it? You're the disgusting one, Derek. Tucking your penis away, putting on tights and makeup. It's absurd. It's wrong.

The masked man starts to masturbate with one hand. He flexes the fingers of his other hand and then balls them into a tight fist.

A knocking can be heard offstage.

MARY (offstage): Cassie, it's me. Are you ready to go?

CASSANDRA: The door's open. Come in.

A thumping sound offstage.

MARY (offstage): It won't open. Is there something blocking the door?

Cassandra looks at the masturbating masked man.

CASSANDRA: So he is real. I thought I was going insane!

DIANE: Oh not this again, Derek.

CASSANDRA: Mum, he's standing right there next to you! He's blocking the door and wanking off!

Diane gets to her feet.

DIANE: I've had enough of you. You're a crude, disgusting boy. I want you out of my house.

CASSANDRA: So do I, but there's a fat bloke having a wank in your doorway!

DIANE: You've gone mad. You've lost the plot!

Cassandra steps towards Diane and places a hand on her shoulder.

CASSANDRA: Mum, just look—

DIANE: —Don't you touch me. You're a disgusting, vile boy!

Diane shrugs Cassandra off and exits stage left. She returns, holding a kitchen knife. Diane points it at Cassandra.

DIANE: I told you to get out. You disgust me. I can't stand to look at you anymore. Just get out.

CASSANDRA: Seriously? A fucking knife? You're threatening me with a knife?

DIANE: Don't you swear at me, boy. If you get angry like that, God knows what else you'll do.

CASSANDRA: You're the one holding a fucking knife at your own daughter.

DIANE: I don't have a daughter!

Diane closes the gap between them and waves the knife in Cassandra's face. The masked man locks the door behind him and steps behind Cassandra. He wraps one arm around her neck, his erect penis pressing against her back.

MARY (knocking): Cassie? Are you okay? I can hear shouting.

DIANE: You want to be a girl so badly, why don't I cut it off for you? You'd probably thank me, wouldn't you?

The man's arm tightens around Cassandra's throat and he thrusts his penis back and forth against her back. With his free hand, he reaches around and rubs at her chest.

DIANE: Filthy, crude, perverted boy.

The sound of a window smashing. Mary enters from the kitchen, stage left.

MARY: Cassie! Get your fucking hands off her.

Mary snatches the knife from Diane's hand and shoves her backwards. Diane tumbles back into the armchair.

Cassandra thrusts an elbow back into the ribs of the masked man, and he releases her. She takes the knife from Mary and jabs it into the man's crotch, ripping through his penis and scrotum. Blood drips onto the stage.

MARY: *Come on.*

Mary takes Cassandra's hand, unlocks the door behind the man, and the pair exit stage right.

The masked man pulls the knife from his penis and thrusts it into Diane's chest, then exits stage left. Diane dies, and the curtain falls.

[Director's note: I don't like this ending. There's no way Cassandra could overpower such a big guy. We should fix this. Maybe have him throw her to the floor and have his way with her first. Then Mary and Diane could team up to kill him? We'll talk about it before rehearsals start.]

WE UNDERSTAND EACH OTHER PERFECTLY

Mel had been walking this tree-lined stretch of road for over an hour before someone eventually stopped.

The woman who pulls over is middle-aged, probably just past fifty. Her greying hair is tied up in a loose bun, and her nails are painted all different colours. Her car is large enough for a family but she is driving alone. Her name is Eleanor.

"Need some help?" Eleanor asks after winding down the driver's side window.

"I'm hoping to get to London," says Mel.

"Well, I'm not going quite that far but near enough. And hey, maybe if I like you, I'll take you all the way." She flashes a friendly smile. "Hop in."

"Thanks," Mel squeaks. She jogs around the back of the car, drops her bag on the back seat, and climbs in next to Eleanor.

"You seem pretty young to be doing something so risky," says Eleanor after she pulls away and back onto the road.

"You're not wrong," says Mel, fixing her seatbelt, "but I didn't know what else to do."

"Okay, so, let me guess..."

"You'll probably guess right," says Mel, dragging her index fingers back and forth across the bags under her eyes and massaging her temples.

"Running away from home?"

"Yup."

"I did the same thing at your age."

"Really? Is that why you stopped to pick me up?"

Eleanor smiled her charming smile again. "Kindred spirits."

Mel smiled into her lap and tucked a loose strand of hair behind her ear.

"How long were you walking for before I came along?"

"Quite a while, actually. I started in Worcester."

"Oh wow, you must've been walking all day!"

"Yeah, I set out this morning before my parents woke up."

"Smart."

"I didn't want to leave in the middle of the night. I thought, wait until sunrise, y'know? Then get out in that little window of time before they get up."

"Sounds like you know what you're doing."

Mel laughs at that. "I certainly hope so."

"My name's Eleanor, by the way."

"I'm Mel. Thanks again for giving me a lift."

"No problem at all. Like I said, kindred spirits." Eleanor

turns to Mel and flashes her another quick grin.

"So, why did you run away when you were my age?"

Eleanor snickers. "A boy. Isn't that so often the way? My parents didn't want me going out with him so I decided to leave so I could make my own decisions."

"Did you and him run away together?"

"Oh, God, no, he wouldn't have done that for me. Not in a million years. No, this was a principal thing. If my dad thought he had a say in my love life—if he thought he could control my decisions—then I didn't want to live under his roof."

"I totally get that. How old were you?"

"Probably seventeen? Yeah, seventeen."

"I'm eighteen."

"Not at university?"

"I mean, that was the plan for a while, but life got complicated and I didn't feel like I was in the right headspace for it. Not yet, at least. I'd like to go but I need to figure myself out first."

"That's smart. Very mature."

"You think so? Even the running-away-from-home part?"

"We all have our reasons for why we do what we do. And it sounds to me like anyone who has thought that sensibly about their situation and their future must have a decent reason for wanting to get out." Eleanor scratches her nose and swallows. "I won't pry, by the way. You don't need to tell me why you decided to run. Like I said, I've been there."

"Did it go well for you, in the end?"

Eleanor sucks her teeth and clicks her tongue. "That's a big question. Yes and no. My life definitely took a different path after I did that, and who's to say what it would've looked like if I had stayed put."

"I guess we can all wonder that."

"True, true, true enough. You can look back on any big choice and wonder where the other road would've led you."

Mel nods, watching the passing trees. "Exactly."

Eleanor reaches with one hand into her bag. "Hungry? I've got some chocolate here."

"Oh, sure, I won't say no. Thanks." Mel takes the chocolate bar gently and unwraps it.
"You never know when you'll get a craving or just feel a bit peckish, so I've always got some chocolate on me somewhere. Sweet tooth."

After swallowing the last bite, Mel giggles and says, "If I'd been picked up by a man instead, and he'd have offered me chocolate, I probably wouldn't have taken it."

Eleanor laughs at that. "Absolutely, good girl. You learn those lessons quickly, huh?"

"I mean, I've never actually been hurt by a guy. Not physically. But—"

"—But that doesn't make them trustworthy. Men often want a medal just for not causing any physical harm to a woman, like there's something courageous in that. But it's not enough, is it? Men don't even know us—what we go through—let alone respect us."

"Are you married?"

"Do I sound married?"

"I guess not."

"Well, plot twist! I actually am. My husband's a good egg, though. One of the few good ones, I reckon. But they're out there. I found mine, after all. A man who understands what men are really like, and so he treats me with real respect. Always has. He's a decent feminist, I think—he'd have to be, to put up with me!—and we've raised our kids just the same."

"How many do you have?"

"Two, both girls, both in primary school."

"That's lovely." Mel offers Eleanor a polite smile. "I'm glad you found one of the good guys."

"Me too. They're like hen's teeth. Any boys on your radar? Or girls? No judgement."

"Uh, no, I haven't found the time to worry about that side of things."

"I appreciate that," says Eleanor. "Work yourself out first, then worry about attaching yourself to someone else. You'll be healthier for it."

"I haven't consciously been doing that but you're right; that's a good way to look at it."

"So, why London?" Eleanor asks after a short period of silence.

"It felt like the most sensible choice. I'll need some help to stay on my feet, and I have friends there. Friends I know from social media and forums and stuff."

"Reckon you can trust them?"

"Oh, definitely, yeah."

"And do you know London yourself?"

"I've visited a few times."

"Okay. I don't disagree that a big city is the most sensible place to go. If you stay in a small town, nothing will happen."

"Yeah, exactly," says Mel, nodding to herself a few times. "London's a liberal place full of all kinds of people. I can find a community there."

"I hope you do," says Eleanor as she flicks at the car's indicator. "There's a service station just here. Fancy stopping for a coffee?"

"Oh, sure. I could use the loo, actually."

Eleanor parks the car and leads the way into the service station. Inside, families are standing in bunches, arguing or laughing; men in suits are queuing for coffee with their arms folded; there is an endless flow of people walking into and out of the bathrooms.

"Coffee?" Eleanor asks. "I'll get you one."

"You don't mind?"

"Not at all."

"Thanks. I'm just going to pop to the loo first." Mel gives a pinched smile and moves to join the flow of people heading that way.

Eleanor jogs up behind and catches Mel. "Hang on, on second thought, I'll come with you. Might as well."

"Sure, long drive."

In the women's, they wait their turns and Mel enters a cubicle when it becomes available. Eleanor takes the one next to it. Mel sits for a moment longer than she needs to, catches her breath, reminds herself that this is right; this is good. She nods to herself a few times, flushes, and unlocks the stall door. She and Eleanor exit their cubicles at the same time, wash their hands next to each other, and leave together.

Eleanor buys them each a latte and a muffin, and they head back out to the car.

"Do you have a licence?" Eleanor asks, resuming their chitchat.

"I took a few lessons but didn't have the money to keep it going."

"That's fair. They're stupidly expensive. And if you end up staying in London, you won't need one."

"Yeah, that's what I figured."

"Look out for yourself when you get there, by the way. Doesn't matter what borough you're in, you need to be sensible when you're out."

"I know."

Eleanor continues anyway. "You're young, and people can tell when you're not used to the city. Especially men. They prey on people who look lost and vulnerable."

"Yeah, I'll do my best to blend in. I'm used to doing that. I'll just keep my head down and look like I always know where I'm going, even if I don't."

"That's a good plan. I like that."

Mel smiles to herself. "I'm hoping to find a community there. Like-minded people I can spend time with."

"What kind of a community?"

"Y'know, just people who are like me. Who like the same stuff."

"And what kind of stuff is that?"

"Just…" Mel searches for the right words. "…the same

kinds of music. Books. Video games. People who share the same views as me about things."

"Like religion and politics? That kind of thing?"

"Right," says Mel. "Exactly."

"Well, you sound like a pretty liberal person. You consider yourself a feminist?"

"Oh, absolutely, yes. I've read plenty of feminist writers and I really don't like spending too much time around guys."

"So, you *do* like girls then?"

Mel pauses before she answers. "I think I like both, but I struggle finding good male friends, let alone a boyfriend."

"Men are hard to love," says Eleanor. "But when you find the right one, you keep a hold of him."

"Right. Well, I guess I'll see what happens when I get to London."

"I guess you will."

"I just realised I haven't asked why you're heading this way."

"Oh! I'm just off visiting a friend. She lives in Hampshire."

"That's lovely. Are you old friends?"

"Yep," says Eleanor. "We go right back to secondary school. She's been through a lot in her life so I check in on her pretty frequently."

"Is she doing okay now?"

"I think so. She just got out of yet another difficult relationship. It gets to a point where you wonder if she's seeking them out on purpose, y'know? Like she's out there asking for trouble."

"So this has become a kind of pattern for her?"

"Definitely." Eleanor nods and scratches at her scalp through her bunned-up hair. "All the way back to her early twenties, actually. She liked bad boys. Thought she could fix them, tame them, whatever. Her first boyfriend was literally in a gang. He hit her once and she was smart enough to walk away. But then it happened again. Another bad boy. So then she moves onto more stable men. Men with good jobs; men who get up early to go to the gym. Men who spend the weekend doing cultured stuff like going to see a play or walking around a museum. These relationships would last a few months and then the cracks would start to show. One guy cheated on her, another threatened her. And on it goes." She sighs slowly. "Fuck men."

"Wow, I'm so sorry. It's not easy to tell the good from the bad where men are concerned."

"Absolutely. That's why I'm grateful I found my husband. But her string of bad luck has lasted for decades. At this point, I don't know how she finds the strength to trust men at all. She never stays single for long. There's always another one on the horizon. I mean, she was actually engaged for a while in her thirties. They moved in together, things were great."

"What happened?"

"It wasn't one single thing. He started pulling her away from her friends, telling her things that made her not want to spend as much time with them. He'd tell her she'd be better off just with him. Then he started getting her to try certain diets, telling her she was getting fat, letting herself go."

"Sounds like gaslighting."

"Is that what it is?"

"Yeah, maybe. Look it up later and see if it sounds right."

"Yeah, well, whatever it was, it kept her and I apart for quite a few months. When she started feeling alone and exhausted by it all, she bit back. She would stand up to him, and that would rile him up. So he would stand over her, intimidate her, remind her that he's bigger and stronger. Men like him love letting us know that we're the weaker sex. And eventually, she had to sneak out of the house while he was at work, and she came straight to me for help. She ended up leaving a lot of her things behind but it was worth it to get away from him."

"Jesus, what a psycho."

"Yeah."

"I'm glad she's rid of him. And that she's got you for support."

"Well, there have been others since. She still hasn't learned not to trust men."

"I mean, she's a lonely person who likes men. What can she do except keep dating and hope that she finds the right one?"

"Nothing, I suppose." Eleanor shrugs and taps at the steering wheel. "But she's better off on her own, in my opinion."

Mel sniffs and looks down at her lap. "What needs to change is the culture around men's treatment of women. They grow up believing the narrative that they can do what they want, say what they like, go where they please, hurt whoever they feel like hurting. I do think it's changing slowly but not fast enough."

"I'm not sure men can change. If a man wants to hurt a woman, he just can. He has that freedom. He knows he's stronger, and he likes that fact, I think. It's in his bones to hurt a woman. Sometimes it feels like men are our natural predators. They like hurting us. And if a man wants to cheat on his woman, it's easy. Nobody's ever told him it's bad to do that. He doesn't see any reason not to, and it's not hard to charm a half-drunk, half-dressed young girl on a night out."

"Isn't that kind of patronising the girl though?"

Eleanor scoffs. "She doesn't know any different, does she. But she will. She'll get hurt and then she'll learn."

Mel says nothing for a moment, then: "I'm sorry your friend has gone through so much."

"Me, too." Eleanor's knuckles turn white as she strangles the steering wheel.

"Here's a plan," says Eleanor. "We're getting close to my friend's place, and I'm pretty sure she lives close to a station with a regular train that goes straight to London. The journey can't be more than an hour from there. Why don't you come in with me, have a cup of tea, relax for a bit, and then Helen can show you how to get to the station. I think it's a pretty short walk."

"Sure, that sounds great. Thank you. You sure she won't mind me dropping in?"

"Not at all. She's great at baking, too, so you'll probably get some cake or a sausage roll or something. You veggie or vegan?"

"Nope. Love meat."

"Me too."

"Hello-o," Eleanor calls as she opens the front door.

"He-ey," Helen replies in the exact same tone. She comes around the corner from the living room and embraces Eleanor in a long hug before taking Eleanor's overnight bag and placing it on the stairs.

Helen is Eleanor's age, her greying hair dyed blonde. She's shorter than Eleanor, and wears an infectious smile.

Eleanor and Mel, crammed into the narrow hallway by the door, remove their shoes and follow Helen into her living room. As they walk, Eleanor says: "Helen, this is Mel. I picked her up on the side of the road, believe it or not."

Helen laughs politely, then stops and looks from Mel to Eleanor. "Are you serious?"

Eleanor chuckles. "Yep!"

Mel nods and forces a pinched smile. "Hi. Sorry for intruding. Your house is lovely."

"Oh, thank you. Please, take a seat. What were you doing on the side of the road?"

"I left home this morning and thought hitchhiking would be cheaper than a train."

"And more dangerous, too!" Helen exclaims. "You're lucky it was Ellie who picked you up and not someone dangerous."

Mel nods in agreement. "She's been very kind, giving me a lift all this way."

"I told her you'd help guide her to the station in a bit," says Eleanor. "She wants to get into London."

Oh, sure, no problem at all," says Helen. "Quick and easy from here. Do you both want some tea? And I've just made sausage rolls."

Eleanor taps Mel's arm with a knuckle. "Didn't I tell you?"

"Yeah," says Mel softly, "that would all be lovely, thank you."

"Great, two seconds and I'll be back."

After Helen leaves the room, Mel takes in the room and says: "She's really nice."

"She's great, isn't she? Like I said, a bad track record with men but it hasn't made her jaded. She's still an angel."

Mel spots a purple, white, and green sticker in the corner of the living room window, facing outside. "Isn't that the suffragette flag?"

"Good eye," says Eleanor. "We go to a lot of rallies in London together. Justice for abuse victims, support for homeless women, keeping men out of women's spaces. That kind of thing."

"That's great," says Mel.

"It's important," says Eleanor. "Men will do anything they can to attack and abuse women, even engaging in sick sexual fetishes like dressing up like us."

Helen returns with a floral metal tray covered with mugs and small plates. "Are you talking about the marches?"

"Yep," says Eleanor as she helps Helen put the tray down on the coffee table. "Just telling Mel what kinds of perverted things men will do to get close to vulnerable women."

"Oh, yes," says Helen as she passes Mel a steaming cup of tea. "The twisted ways men think. You know, some of them are so sick in the head that they'll actually dress up in women's clothing in order to get into our bathrooms and changing rooms."

"Is that right?" Mel asks before blowing at the steam from her cup.

Eleanor slaps a hand down onto her thigh. "You must have seen it on the news, Mel. Some of these men even take *our* hormones to make them look more feminine. And their bloody GPs just hand these pills out to them like sweets! The NHS is enabling these abusers."

Mel takes a long sip of her tea as she listens.

"That was what the last rally we went to was all about, wasn't it? Calling out the NHS for siding with these trannies and their sick fetishes." She laces her fingers together and looks Mel in the eye. "Trannies like you."

Mel's eyes spring open and she almost spills her tea. "Excuse me?"

"Don't pretend, Mel. Or whatever your *actual* name is. I knew from the moment I saw you on the side of the road. Do you really think you're managing to fool anyone?"

"I don't know what you mean."

"What's your real name?" Helen asks.

"Mel," says Mel, with a shudder in her voice.

"Right," says Eleanor, "we'll just call you *boy* then, shall we?"

Helen laughs. "Let me guess, boy, you make a little game

of dressing up like that and pretending to hitchhike until a kindly woman, driving all alone, offers to pick you up, and then you do whatever you want with her. How many women have you already hurt?"

"But I didn't do that," says Mel, staring hard into her teacup. "I haven't done anything. To anyone."

"Not yet," says Eleanor. "You never would've left here without attacking and raping us both."

"What? No! I just wanted a lift to London. I'll just go right now and leave you both alone."

Mel moves to stand up and is hit with a painful headrush.

"Enjoy your tea?" Helen asks. Mel sits back down slowly and blinks to clear her vision. "You're not leaving here, boy. We can't have sick freaks like you out on the street, dressing like us and preying on innocent women who don't know any better." Helen looks across to Eleanor. "What should we do with this one?"

"The last one had the bathtub, and to be honest I didn't love it. Wasn't very satisfying."

"That's fair. He was ugly, too. All that stubble." Helen laughs. "This one is definitely more convincing, I'll give him that."

"It's those shoulders, though. And have you seen his Adam's apple?" They both laugh this time. "Go get your garden shears. We'll have some fun pulling this one apart."

Helen hops to her feet and leaves the room quickly.

"Right," says Eleanor, gripping Mel's leg tight, her fingers digging into the girl's flesh. "Tell me now: how many women have you already hurt?"

It takes effort for Mel to swallow the lump of spit that has clogged in her throat. The room is spinning and her stomach is churning. "None," she says eventually.

The slap comes quick and hard. "Liar!" Eleanor hisses. "This is going to hurt so much more if you don't tell us the truth, you filthy little pervert. Who have you already hurt?"

"Mel blinks back tears. "Nobody. I don't want to hurt anyone."

Another slap; this one harder. "Liar," Eleanor shouts again. "Pervert. Rapist. Freak."

"I'm just a girl who wants to get to London."

Eleanor grabs a handful of Mel's hair and yanks her head backwards, forcing her to face the ceiling. "You're no girl, you rotten animal. You're a mentally ill little creep. You should be locked up or killed."

"Fortunately," says Helen as she returns with a pair of shears, a metal dish, and a towel, "you've come to the right place for that." She kneels down in front of the sofa on which Mel and Eleanor are sitting. "What should we take first?"

Eleanor laughs. "What else? Snip his cock off."

Mel manages to squirm against whatever drug is keeping

her weak and dizzy, but not enough to stop Helen from tugging at her jeans until they give way and start to slide down. "Why are you doing this?" she asks in a sobbing grunt.

"Shut up," says Helen as she pulls Mel's jeans past her knees.

"This is revenge for all the women you and your kind have ever hurt," Eleanor whispers in Mel's ear. "All the witches you burned. All the rape and abuse and murder."

"But I'm a woman," says Mel, tears running down her cheek. "I'm on your side. I've never hurt anyone."

Helen takes the pliers in one hand and grabs at Mel's underwear with the other, but before she can do anything else, Mel's knee comes up to meet her chin. Helen lets out a grunt and tumbles backwards, hitting her head hard on the coffee table's edge and leaving a crimson smear. Despite the urge to vomit and pass out, Mel only needed one good shot, and she took it. Adrenaline can perform little miracles, as Mel is quickly learning.

"Bastard!" Eleanor shouts as she raises a hand to swipe at Mel's face. She is stopped mid-swing as Mel takes a hold of her wrist and bends her arm back until her elbow pops. Eleanor's head jolts back as she lets out an agonised scream which exposes the white skin of her neck. While still holding the screaming woman's wrist, Mel sinks her teeth into Eleanor's neck and rips away a chunk of flesh. Blood pours out, and Eleanor's pale skin turns whiter still. Mel spits Eleanor's skin back into her face before punching her square on the nose, knocking her out and leaving her to bleed on the sofa.

Helen is dazed but awake. Blood has matted the hair on one side of her head. She flails a little, attempting to focus her vision and steady herself on the floor. She blinks a few times and frowns at Mel as she gets herself up off the sofa.

"What…" is all that Helen is able to say. She continues to blink and frown and whimper and pull herself into a sitting position, her back against the table.

Mel squats down in front of the concussed woman, her heart thumping quick and hard against her ribs—the adrenaline is all that's keeping her upright. "You see what happens when you hunt us? Like witches? Eventually, the scapegoats bite back. Now, how many trans girls have you killed already?"

Helen can only whimper in response. Mel isn't even sure if she's lucid. With nothing else to do, she sighs and picks up Helen's discarded shears from the living room floor. Grabbing a handful of Helen's hair, just as Eleanor had done to her, Mel yanks Helen's head backwards and jams the pliers into the side of her neck. They sink in deep. A fountain of blood gushes out, staining the table and the carpet red. Helen gasps for air, but it isn't enough, and she loses consciousness quickly. Almost too quickly.

Mel straightens up and looks at the blood-soaked bodies. She sighs and wipes the blood from her face and hands with Helen's teatowel. "All I wanted was a lift into London."

BABY

Hey.

Hi.

Sorry to call out of the blue—

—No, it's fine, I don't mind.

You sure? 'Cause I get it if—

—No, really, it's fine. What's up?

It's just that I'm visiting my parents at the moment and I had this weird thing happen yesterday and it got me thinking.

What was the weird thing? Are they being decent?

Actually yeah, they're okay this time. It's not even about them. It was just how, like, you know how old places get stuck in time and you don't expect them to change?

Yeah?

There's been a really big change. A kind of trippy one.

Okay, now I'm intrigued.

Right, so I've been here for a few days, and so yesterday I decided to go for a walk around the village. Y'know, I grew up here and nothing has ever changed but, anyway, you remember when you visited me a while back and I showed you where my grandparents used to live? The little house where my mum grew up?

Yeah, it's in that little dip in the village? Almost like a valley?

Yeah, right down the bottom of that bumpy lane. Just a pair of really old stone cottages, right?

Right.

So, you might not have noticed but that whole lane, that dip is surrounded by overgrown shrubbery and stuff. And behind all that is a lot of marshland. It's all stagnant ponds and streams that don't go anywhere. And paths that you can't walk down anymore since they got taken over by brambles and bushes and whatever else. And it's always just been like that, ever since my mum was a kid. She said it's gotten worse over time, like, more out of control and overgrown, and nobody does anything about it—I guess they don't care—but the gross ponds and marshy land has just always been there. Just… it just sits and stagnates.

Okay?

Well, I took a walk around there yesterday and it's all gone! It's transformed! This enormous area of marshy land is now— I can't believe I'm saying this—it's all luxury condos and a big, massive graveyard.

It's what? Condos for who? And who builds a fresh graveyard?

Right? And it's really huge, too. The graveyard, I mean. So, now you've got this pair of old stone cottages at the bottom of a lane, surrounded on almost all sides by really nice apartment blocks with floor-to-ceiling windows and balconies.

And there's this rise that I didn't even know was there because of the overgrowth. It's this huge hillside sort of climbing up out of the valley, and that's where the graveyard is! The graves just pepper this whole hillside. Hundreds of them. It's insane!

Has the graveyard always been there? Or is it new?

That was what I wondered as well.

And who's living in luxury condos all the way out there?

So, those questions kind of go together. There's this flat bit of manicured grass outside two of the buildings, kind of like a green or a miniature park or whatever. And some people were sat on benches there just chatting to each other. I said hi and asked them about the condos.

What did they say?

They said that some of them are occupied by retired people who wanted to just escape to the countryside. Standard, I guess. But a lot of the residents are gravediggers. The graveyard, it turns out, *is* new. So, we do build new graveyards, I guess. That's a thing. Who knew! And this graveyard is huge and, so these guys said, it's going to be super popular. So the council built these nice new flats for all the gravediggers and caretakers to live in.

Wow, that's a lot. And they said the graveyard is going to be popular... That's a bit weird, isn't it?

I literally thought the same when he told me. That's why the word stuck in my head. Popular.

And why there, on a big hillside in a little English village?

Honestly, I've got no idea. That's pretty much all I learned. This quiet village now has a bunch of luxury condos occupied by retired Londoners or whatever, and a bunch of men who take care of an enormous new graveyard. Insane, right?

Yup. I honestly don't know what to say.

I didn't either. Just kinda left after that. So, how—*uh*—how's the baby?

He's… a little worse than he was, to be honest. He's been running a bit of a fever for two days, and his eyes won't stop streaming.

Is that, like, a side effect of the blindness?

Doctor's not sure. She's also not sure what the fluid actually is. It has this milky white colour.

Oh.

Yeah. So she gave me some medicine to tackle the fever and said to come back soon if his eyes get worse. In case it's an infection, I guess.

Could an infection have caused the blindness?

No, Leane. He was born blind.

Right. Sorry.

It's okay.

No, I mean, like, about everything.

About leaving?

I haven't left for good. I just needed time to think.

To think about leaving.

No, I—

—It's okay, I do get it. Really. It's a lot of responsibility. It was my choice. And dads leave. It's what they do.

I'm not a dad, Emma.

But you are, though. You're not a man but you're still Jack's dad.

I guess you're right.

Just stay with your parents a little longer. Keep thinking. And I'll understand, whatever decision you make.

———··•··———

Leane.

Hm?

I need your help. Were you asleep?

Was kinda just dropping off. What's wrong?

It's Jack.

Has his fever gotten worse? Is it an infection?

It's, I don't know, he's... his eyes are... they're not right.

Want me to come to you?

No, it's late, I just panicked and—

—Call the doctor. Or I can do it. But I don't really know what to say to her. I'm not there.

His eyes are just wrong. Like... they don't look like eyes anymore. They're not wet or glassy. They're just balls of... meat? Skin? They look like... tumours.

What?

They're just two sickly, awful-looking things in his head. It's not right, Leane. I don't—

—Please call the doctor right now, and then tell me what she says. I'm hanging up.

—— ··•·· ——

What did she say?

A lot. It's a lot.

Okay?

I described his eyes to her and she sounded worried. Like she couldn't disguise it, y'know? And then she had me take a photo of him and send it to her. I heard her gasp, Leane.

So it's bad? Is he really sick?

She says they're cysts. His eyes. They're not eyes; they're cysts. The stuff that was leaking from them, it's like puss or something. Leane, he's got two cysts where his eyes should be.

How is that even possible?

She asked me about you. She asked who the father is, and so I told her. She asked a bunch of questions about you and when I finally mentioned that you're trans, she went quiet.

What does that have to do with anything?

The doctor said that Jack isn't the first one. That getting someone pregnant while you're on oestrogen, it does something to the baby.

Does what?

This! It does this, Leane!

That's bullshit. That's absolute bollocks. Being a trans parent is nothing new! Why would something like this be happening now, all of a sudden? No, that's bullshit. She must be some kind of TERF. There's plenty of them in the NHS. I had to go through so much—

—I know what you went through, but this is just what she said. She said it has *happened before. A few times. Recently. Babies born with these awful deformities, and the only connection is that their fathers were all taking oestrogen.*

I don't believe it.

Leane, listen, I know this is upsetting for you. You're probably offended or whatever. But I have a sick baby next to me and his fever is getting worse and I don't know what to do.

Did the doctor not tell you what to do?

She said she wasn't sure. She said the cysts can't be removed yet because he's too small, but they also might get bigger and that's really dangerous because they're in his head. I think they're painful. They're hurting him.

So… what do we do?

I don't know. He's asleep now. But his eyes are bulging. If the cysts get bigger, he won't be able to close his eyelids.

Fuck. Well, if he's sleeping now, why don't you get some sleep and call me tomorrow if anything changes. Actually, either way, I'll drive home.

No, you don't have to. You being here won't change anything.

But I want to be there.

Okay, well, we can talk tomorrow.

Right, okay, just get some sleep.

I'll try. You, too.

Emma? What time is it? Jesus, it's past midnight.

How big is that graveyard?

What?

Are there any unoccupied graves?

I don't understand.

I don't think it was the oestrogen. It can't have been.

I knew it. It would be impossible. It makes no sense.

But she did say he's not the first.

I don't care what she said. Anyway, how is he right now?

I think I need to bring him to you.

What do you mean? I mean, yeah, you can, but why?

There are these… holes in his arms.

Holes?

They look just like eye sockets. They opened up in his skin overnight. They're these oval-shaped things. Black inside. It's like his... flesh has been scooped out. They look just like empty eye sockets. And they're all up and down his arms.

I don't—

—*It's true, Leane.*

Okay, I believe you.

And the cysts have gotten bigger, and they're leaking more. He can't close his eyes, Leane. Oh, God.

You have to take him to the hospital right now.

He can't close his eyes, but he's not crying. He just stares at me. I know he can't see, and that they're not eyes, but he still just stares at me with them.

Is he eating?

Yes.

Okay. I don't know what else to say.

Neither do I.

Why did you ask about the graveyard?

If I bring him to you, we could—

—What? We could what, Emma? Bury him?

I don't know, I just—

You have to take him to a hospital!

I'm scared. I'm too scared. What's wrong with our baby, Leane?

I don't know. That's why you have to take him. Don't call the doctor again. Take him straight to A&E or something.

I don't know.

I'm not there to do it for you. Fuck's sake, I knew I should've driven back. Okay, I'm getting in my car now. I'll be there soon.

No, I'm coming to you! Don't go anywhere because I'm putting him in my car right now.

Okay, fine. Fine.

———··•··———

Leane.

Are you on your way?

Yeah, about halfway there.

How is he?

He's just, he's just watching me. From the backseat. I'm watching him in the rearview mirror.

He doesn't have eyes, Emma.

He does! They're all eyes, and they're all watching me. I can see them moving and blinking.

It's just in your head. You're panicking, maybe in shock or something? Make sure you drive carefully. Don't rush. I should've come to get you, I'm sorry.

There wouldn't have been time.

Time for what?

He's getting worse. His eyes… the cysts are bulging. And I swear, there's this, this shadow.

Shadow?

It's a thing. It's attached to him, like a shadow, but it's not a shadow. And it moves before he does.

It's just a trick of the passing streetlamps. It's late, the lights and the shadows do funny things.

Right, yeah. You're right. Okay.

Call me when you're two minutes away and I'll come outside to meet you.

Okay.

Are you here?

I'm driving down to the graveyard.

What? Why?

He's... dangerous, Leane. He's growing.

Growing?

Getting bigger, yes. And the shadow thing—

—Isn't real, Emma. It isn't.

It is! It moves, and it flashes, like it's blinking, and then Jack... he looks at me. The holes in his arms, they stare at me. He isn't speaking. The cysts, they're weeping, and I can feel them looking at me, too. He's possessed or something.

There's no such thing! He's sick. We need to take him to a hospital.

No, no. No. Meet me at the graveyard. I'm almost there. You don't have a choice.

———··●··———

Emma!

He's in the car. I need help getting him out. He's too big.

Oh my god, you're right. Oh, Jack, no. What happened—

—*I told you! He's not... he's not our baby.*

He is, he's... he's just sick.

Just help me get him out.

And then what? We throw him in a ditch? He's our child, Emma!

I don't think he is.

I'm not listening to this. Get in the passenger seat. I'll drive us to the hospital.

No, wait! There's a man. Over there, look. On that bench.

Is he looking at us?

I think so.

Okay, wait here.

— ··●·· —

What did he want? What did he say?

He said we're not the first. The graves. They were dug for us.

What?

Jack's doctor said he wasn't the first, right? That gravedigger just said the same, that doctors have been sending parents of kids like Jack here, to be disposed of.

Disposed of?

You wanted to do it! You had the same idea.

But the idea that this is part of some plan.

The man said it's not a plan, it's an epidemic of kids born cursed. By people like me.

You told me that was bollocks.

Well, what am I supposed to believe now, Emma? He said there are graves here filled with the deformed babies of trans parents! We fucked up!

I don't believe it.

Look at our son! I did this!

No, you didn't. Someone else did. This isn't on us. Someone else is to blame for this. Someone must be tampering with the babies of trans parents. In order to make trans people look like monsters. Right? To make you think you're a monster!

You can't just make up conspiracy theories on the spot like that.

Tell me it doesn't make sense.

Who would have done this to Jack? And how?

I don't know, but it makes no less sense than him being deformed by oestrogen-tainted jizz, does it!

So you're thinking the government or the NHS is deforming babies to make the country think trans parents are literally poisonous?

Yes!

Right, well, we can't think about this now. We have to decide what we do with Jack.

You said that these graves were put here for him. That the graveyard is full of other kids like Jack.

That doesn't mean we should do what they did.

Leane, he's not… right. He's sick and I think he's dangerous.

How?

The shadow—

—Isn't real.

Yes it is! Help me get him out of the car and you'll see.

Oh my god, he's so heavy.

Don't touch his arms.

I don't want to.

Do you see the shadow?

That's just *his* shadow.

Bring him into the light. Here, the headlamps.

Oh… what is that?

It's something evil. It makes… shapes, and then Jack mimics them. The eyes on his arms, they stare at you.

Have you got a tissue? His eyes are weeping.

They're not eyes, remember? And the weeping doesn't stop.

Fuck, I actually saw it. The shadow thing.

Come on, help me get him to a grave.

This is awful. Why are we doing this? How have you found the strength?

I've been watching him change for days. He's not our little boy anymore. Whatever we end up burying, it isn't Jack.

You've already made your peace with this?

I've had to. It's the truth.

Ow!

What happened?

He bit me. *Ah*, that's a lot of blood.

And he's still getting bigger.

What is that?

It's the shadow thing.

It doesn't want us to bury him.

We have to. Grab that shovel.

His shadow's writhing… squirming. What's happening?

Leane, get him off me! Fuck, get him off!

I'm trying!

Push him in!

No, you'll fall.

Do it! Push him in!

LITTLE BLUE STICKY NOTES

Part 1

My husband died last week.

He was, so the police told me, on his way back from the pub. It was a Friday night, and solo trips to the pub had become the norm for him by now—by then. I always looked forward to them.

He would leave after dinner, head out on foot, and walk the half-mile to *The Crooked Man*. There, he would sit, drink, and—I assume—make chit-chat with the other ratty-looking middle-aged men who habitually hug the bar. This had morphed into his Friday night routine some years ago, and it remained mostly unchanged. Last Friday, however, he stumbled home in the dark and was hit by a car. It had crossed my mind more than once how something that was possible; that it could happen. Eventually. How many times have you been driving at night and been shocked at the sight of someone walking alone along the verge, wearing dark colours and carrying no torch? That was what he did, and eventually his luck ran out.

It was a hit-and-run, so the police told me. They examined the crime scene and are currently entertaining the question of whether or not the driver was also drunk. There were skid marks, which imply the driver likely attempted to stop, but far too late to avoid my black-clad husband. The shape and track of the marks suggests erratic behaviour, and that might have meant they were drunk. The tracks also showed no evidence that the car actually stopped. They might have hit him, thought for a moment about stopping, but then wondered what it might mean for them—prison, probably—and so they just kept on driving into the night. Or maybe they were so drunk that they hardly noticed him at all. Maybe it didn't register that they had hit anyone at all, or if they did, maybe they assumed it was a deer or a dog.

I don't know. What I do know is that my husband is dead, and I am relieved.

Things weren't always so bad between us. There was a time when he showed some affection and occasional tenderness. He would bring home flowers at the end of a workday. He would take me out to a new restaurant he had spotted in town. But that all faded quickly enough, and it was replaced with apathy and routine; then, eventually, violence.

I work from home. I run an arts-and-crafts company that's nothing more than one person (me) knitting and crocheting—occasionally cross-stitching—original and custom pieces and shipping them off to customers all around the world. It doesn't make me rich. In fact, I can just about afford the rent on a studio flat in the city, which is what I'm moving into in just a few weeks. Right now, I'm packing up our house, which sits nestled at the edge of a small town not too far outside London. It's a nice place; I'll be sad to leave it, but I can't afford it by myself.

My husband had been the bread-winner, as he liked to say. He brought home two-thirds of our income, and reminded me of that fact a lot in the early days, when I would buy myself something new or get my hair done. *And where's that money coming from?* he would ask *Because it's certainly not out of your purse, is it?*

That was how it started, looking back. Those comments would be thrown out from time to time, but then we'd go out for a nice dinner. He liked to treat me. And the thing about change is that it rarely happens quickly, but rather in little stages— increments—over time. You might not notice them at first, or at all. The dinners, the weekend breaks, the gifts; time between them gradually expanded until they stopped altogether. It's like weaning yourself off a drug: you adjust to it slowly, over time, until, at last, life seems perfectly normal without it. But without the drug, the pain becomes noticeable. The crass comments, the distrust, the belittling, the questioning. They were my new normal.

I'm not really in the business of excuses. A bitter part of me—which has grown larger and larger, like a cancer, over the years—doesn't want to search for excuses. But the rational part of me knows that anything can be traced backwards. Abusive behaviour can be caused by trauma, anxiety, mental illness, a feeling of displacement. I can say that to myself, like I'm my own psychiatrist, but it doesn't mean anything when you're the one being threatened, being belittled, being hit. He once took me by the wrist and pressed my palm against the electric hob on our stove top because I ruined dinner. You can rationalise that away by tracing his behaviour backwards and figuring out where it all started and why, but that's hard to do when you're screaming; when your skin is blistering and bleeding.

I couldn't work for weeks afterwards, as my hand gradually healed (though I still have the scars, and people ask me about them more than I'd like them to), and he blamed me for our money troubles then. *This is what happens when you don't get a proper job*, he said. *It's inconsistent. You can't work, you don't get money. No sick days, no security, nothing. And now look where we are. Suffering.*

When I told him that I can always leave, that if I'm a burden I can just walk out right now, he laughed, told me to stop playing the victim, and asked me how I could possibly survive without him. *You're stuck with me*, he said.

Those Friday nights when my husband would make his way to the pub, I would take a bath and soothe my soreness. That's where I am now, soaking my thoughts as I plan out what's left to do before the move, which is coming up quickly.

A big van from a local charity is coming in a few days to pick up anything that I want gone. Clothes and shoes and personal effects that belonged to my husband which I have no use for, and some things that were part of our home—furniture, appliances, ornaments, blankets, towels, paintings—that I can't bear to touch or even look at any more.

As a child, I always had an intense relationship with association. I would eat the same meal repeatedly because the first time I had it, I was on holiday. The smell of it would remind me of the beach. I would throw out a CD if I happened to listen to it after a boy broke up with me. It was now tainted and worthless.

Association has fogged up a lot of my life, making me overly reliant on comfort foods, on favourite TV shows and songs. And it also ruins so many things I once loved that I end up having to part with for the sake of my sanity.

Now, even though money is tight, I'm getting rid of so much, in order to defog my brain. On the plus side, I'm moving into a far smaller place, which means that so much of this needs to go regardless.

And so, I've been placing pale pink sticky notes on everything that's mine—everything I want to keep—and blue sticky notes on everything that has to go, everything that's tainted.

Yesterday, I sorted through the wardrobe and placed pink sticky notes on my tops, jeans, skirts, dresses, shoes—even the ones he bought me—and a handbag he gave me for Christmas a few years ago. I thought of getting rid of the things he bought; in fact, I initially decided that I would, as a gut reaction. But as I sat on the bedroom floor and thought, I found that the handbag and some (not all) of the dresses have value that goes beyond him, and so I decided that they can stay after all. If I bring them to my new flat and they start to feel like unwelcome ghosts, I'll just dispose of them.

Blue labels were placed on all of his clothes and shoes, as well as a pair of hiking boots that he bought me when we moved out to this little town. He told me at the time that we should go for long walks and hikes up the hills and along the river. And we did, once. We hiked through the forest until we got to the river, and then we followed it for miles. It was a pleasant walk. At one point, we stopped to skip stones and take photos. We were kneeling at the edge of the water, talking and taking selfies. While he was scrolling back through them, selecting which ones to keep, I scooped up a handful of water and splashed him with it, giggling as I did it, to let him know that I was being playful, that it was just for fun. But he must have seen red. He warned me that I could have broken his phone, and that I would have to buy him a new one, only I couldn't afford to do that, could I? And as he spoke, his rage rose. He got carried away and took me by the back of the neck to dunk my head beneath the water. He stopped suddenly when another hiker appeared over the ridge, and we sat in sharp silence until they passed us. Once they were gone, his rage had dissipated enough that he simply stood up and walked on without waiting for me to follow. When I caught up with him, I threatened to pack my things and leave. He let out an unrestrained belly laugh and asked me where I was planning to go. *You're stuck with me*, he said.

Today, pink labels went on the coffee table, the TV, the bookcase and all the books, one lamp but not the other, and the sofa cushions. Each item has a reason for its colour. I have spent countless peaceful evenings reading by the light of the good lamp, but he threatened more than once to hurl the bad lamp at my head when he assumed I wasn't listening to him.

I stared at the two paintings in the living room. One is an impressionist piece that he always hated and I was excited to keep, and the other is a landscape by a Welsh painter that depicts a farm at sunset and the rolling hills beyond it. We'd had that painting since before moving to this house, and he had often used it as a prop whenever he complained to me about getting out of the city. He would ask me why I couldn't see the appeal of moving, why I was being selfish when I was the one who could work from anywhere. He would jab at the painting and tell me how much better our lives would be in that kind of place. Eventually, he got his wish, and our lives didn't get better. Now, it serves as a bleak reminder of where all of this led us. And it's ugly, to boot.

Tomorrow, I will tackle the kitchen. Stewing in the bath

now, I think about what will be thrown out: the remaining bowls and plates (he smashed too many for me to even look at the ones I have left), the toaster (he once threatened to jam my hand into it), and the microwave (which he once slammed shut with so much force that it no longer closes probably, and is surely as much a health hazard as anything else; I'm not having radiation kill me because of his aggression).

A half-read novel sits unopened on the little table beside me, the steam softening and warping its pages. Next to it, a half-drunk glass of cheap white wine and a half-melted candle on an antique candlestick. My thoughts dance in circles as I wonder what is left to pack, how many more days are needed, how many days I have left, how full the van will be, whether or not two trips might be required, whether or not my new flat will fit all these things, how many new things I'll need to buy and whether or not I can afford them, whether or not I could do without them for the time being, how much money I might save on electric in a small flat, how much I need to save in order to keep a roof over my head, whether or not I might miss this nowhere town, whether or not I should get a cat when I'm settled, whether or not a job might be necessary after all, what friends I might make when I get to London, what men I might meet—

—An almighty crash from the living room echoes up the stairs. It sounds like a china bowl being smashed.

I jolt up, causing water to splash over the edges of the tub and extinguish the candle. I'm in darkness. I sit still, waiting for another noise. There is someone in my house. There has to be. I don't have any pets, and the windows are shut. No bird or bat could have flown in. Someone is in my house.

In the dark, faint outlines of things play tricks on my mind. The sloshing bathwater, the edges of the sink and toilet, the sheen of the mirror. They warp and begin to look unfamiliar, like I am somewhere else, somewhere unfamiliar. I need to move, to turn on the light, to regain my bearings. But if I move, if I turn on the light, whoever is down there will know I'm here. Have they broken in to burgle me? Did they break something by accident in the dark? Is it even dark downstairs? I'm sure I left the lamp on, at least. If it was an accident, they'll be flustered. They might have panicked and fled already. How long have I been sitting here, holding my breath?

I hear no other sounds. The house is so still I can hear the blood pumping through my veins. I can hear the faint sound of wind outside. I have to move. At least, if I get dressed and find something to fight them off with, it's better than being found naked in the tub, vulnerable and undefended.

I stand up and step out of the tub, reaching through the black for a towel and wrapping it around myself. I feel for the candlestick, snatch it, grip it firm, and take slow, gentle steps towards the door. As I open it, I notice that the rest of the house is in darkness. This is not how I left it, I'm sure.

I take a risk and flick on the light at the top of the stairs. I hold my breath and wait to hear footsteps. Something will have been drawn to or chased by the light. But there is still nothing. No sound but the quick thudding of my heart.

I make soft, barefooted steps down the stairs; turn the corner into the short hallway, keeping the light off this time.

I enter the living room, feel for the lightswitch, flick it on, and raise the candlestick like a club.

There's nobody here.

At my feet lies a little blue sticky note, and from it a trail of broken china leading to an exploded lamp, shattered on the floor. The wallpaper just above it has a few fresh cuts across it.

This lamp always sat on the table on the other side of the room. Someone hurled it across the room and smashed it against the wall.

Part 2

It's been three days since I moved into this flat, and still there are boxes full of stuff littering half the floorspace and too many of the surfaces. The boxes, and many of the things inside them, have little pink notes stuck to them. My stuff, all mine. My safety, my comfort. I need to get these things in order.

The problem with unpacking is having to move one box to make space for the things you've removed from another box. It's a loser's Tetris game, and it is exhausting. But every box I empty is an extra bit of free space.

The essentials are done: toiletries and cooking equipment. Now, I'm unpacking anything that can be easily stored or shelved. Clothes, bedding, books, ornaments, framed photos.

I open up the box of pictures. Inside are photos and paintings of various sizes, along with pillows and sofa cushions to keep the pictures padded and safe. I lift out a handful of small photos—scenes from my childhood and my parents on their wedding day—place them on the bookcase behind me, and then pull out the first cushion—a vibrant yellow thing with a pink sticky note attached—and toss it on the sofa. Removing that reveals the impressionist painting that I always loved and my husband always hated. I take it out and immediately hang it pride-of-place on the wall above the TV.

Returning to the box, I lift out another yellow cushion and gasp at what's underneath, my hands moving instinctively to cover my mouth. I try to blink but my eyes won't shut. In the box, with a blue note stuck to it, is the landscape painting my husband loved.

I gave that painting to charity a week ago. It was in a box full of his ugly things, swimming in a sea of little blue sticky notes. Now, it's here. How did I make such a clumsy mistake? What had I been thinking? In the moment, it feels as though my mind is sabotaging me. But I can't afford to entertain thoughts of self-destruction, so I yank the painting from the box, search for a pen, and write *FREE* on the little blue sticky note before taking the painting outside and leaving it beside the building's front door. Someone will give it a home, I'm sure.

Back in the flat, I place the second yellow cushion on the sofa, flat-pack the box, throw it in the recycling, and move on to the next thing.

I tell myself: keep the rhythm, keep focussed on the chores, keep your head empty.

I didn't label the boxes of clothing particularly well. In retrospect, knowing what kinds of clothes were in each cardboard box would have helped me now. As it is, all I can do is pick one at random and start sorting.

I cut through the tape with a knife, pull the box open, and inside I find a random selection of jumpers, blouses, skirts, and a winter coat. I pick out a few drawers and start folding and sorting. I open the wardrobe to hang up the coat on the rail, and notice on the floor of the wardrobe a pair of shoes. No, boots. They must have been left behind by the previous tenant.

I squat down to pick them up, and immediately recognise them. These are the same brand of hiking boots he bought me; ones I threw away before moving. First, I had accidentally brought that awful painting with me, and now I find that the previous tenant has left behind an identical pair of boots that I never wished to see again. I'm beginning to feel cursed; this move is not the clean slate I had hoped for.

I reach into the wardrobe, pick up the boots with one hand, and as I turn them over I find a little blue sticky note stuck to the back of one. I yelp and drop the boots. They tumble to the floor, and the note peels away. It lies on the floor, the phrase *MISS ME?* scrawled across it.

Someone is pulling a horrible prank on me. I stumble into the kitchen, fill a glass with tap water, and try to keep my shaking hand steady as I down the water in one go. But who would want to do this to me? Images of my husband's parents, his brother, and his best friend flash up in my mind. At the funeral, they had all been so sorry. We had shared in our grief, all of us wearing black and playing our parts. His mother and I had both cried and consoled each other, while his brother handed us food and brought up happy memories to try and make us all laugh. It went as funerals go. I mentioned how I would need to downsize, and so I would probably move into a small place in the city. His brother and father had offered to help me move, and I had politely declined. I thought we were on good terms. Was I wrong? Had I been naive? Did they somehow learn of my moving date and decide to sabotage my things? My flat? Plant this stuff amongst my possessions? How many more things would I find as I kept unpacking? And the taunting, childish *"MISS ME?"* written on the sticky note? What brother or friend would dishonour his lost loved one like that? Just to prank me or hurt me? Perhaps my husband wasn't the only malicious member of his family, after all.

My phone rings as I'm refilling the glass. I jump out of my skin and almost drop the glass on the floor. With a still-shaking hand, I place it on the side and pick up my phone.

It's the police. They tell me they have new information about the night of my husband's death. They tell me they have studied the skidmarks, discovered the brand and size of the tyres—as well as which car models would likely match them—enquired at several local garages, and compiled a list of potential suspects. My husband's own car is on the list. I force a laugh and ask how that is possible; they say that it probably means the car that hit him was of a similar size and model as his own—that it is likely a coincidence—but, in the light of this new information, they will need to question me in person at the local police station two days from now. I agree, and hang up.

I refill the glass, gulp down some more water, wash it up, and return it to the cupboard.

As I close the cupboard, I turn and catch a flash of blue out of the corner of my eye. Turning to face the oven and the electric hob, I see a single blue sticky note sitting alone on one of the rings. I take in a shaky breath and step towards it, excited to snatch it away, rip it up, and throw it out. But as I stand over the hob, I see another phrase messily scrawled on the paper: *PLACE HAND HERE*

Tears fill my eyes. I cannot find the strength to reach out and peel away the note. My illogical brain tells me that if I try, some invisible force will press my palm down onto the electric hob, melting the skin of my hand onto the metal plate. This imagined vision has me feeling faint, has my breath rattling in my chest, has me whimpering like a child with a skinned knee. I wrap my arms around myself and step back away from the hob.

After a restless night of tossing and turning—a night of wondering how and why his family or his friends might do this to me, or if perhaps it is someone or something else, and how I'm going to stop it, be free of it, purge myself of this thing that I mustn't call a haunting—I spend this morning unpacking what's left. I'm trying to move swiftly and efficiently, to get the unpacking over with so that I can truly start afresh.

I kneel down on the living room floor and pull open a box labelled "books". I start sorting them by genre and author. Lifting out an armful, I search for their place on the bookcase, slot them in one by one, and repeat.

In amongst the pink-labelled books, I find three of his; each one with a blue sticky note slapped on its cover. This could easily have been an oversight, I tell myself; just me being too hasty and slapdash about packing everything up in time. The first book of his is a nonfiction on the history of Japanese whiskey; the second a crime novel he always took on holiday; the third a book on automation. I grunt, sigh, and throw them in an empty box. More will surely turn up and get thrown out, too. I'm coming to expect it.

More clothes to sort. I fill the chest-of-drawers with underwear, leggings, socks, t-shirts, jumpers. I take an armful of dresses and a jacket, and I move over to the wardrobe. Sliding open the door, my eyes bulge and I let out a sudden scream. Hanging on the rail is my husband's suit; the one he was buried in. Each part of it—trousers, shirt, tie, blazer, and his black shoes placed neatly underneath—is labelled with a little blue sticky note. On each note, the word *MURDERER*

I don't think this is a prank anymore. I can't think that. And yet it still feels like a game, like I'm being toyed with and made to feel frightened. I can almost hear the laughter in my head. I feel as though I am locked in an escape room and being mocked for not knowing how to free myself. It's his laughter I hear. He is enjoying this.

I take down the suit and toss it in the box with the three books.

I cut open each box that hasn't yet been touched. I pull out everything inside and place it all on the floor: every book, blanket, shoe, plate, everything. I take the empty boxes, fold them flat, and take them outside to the recycling bins. I return and grab the box that has his suit and books inside. I seal it shut with tape and drag it outside. I leave it on the pavement and go back inside.

As I slowly unlock the door to my flat, I think about how I will earn my freedom. Once everything is packed away, and all the sticky notes—pink and blue alike—are gone, there will surely be nothing left that could be used to toy with me. Everything that's his will be gone, and everything that's mine will remain. I'll be safe and free and ready to start fresh.

I enter and close the door behind me. I turn the corner and walk into my living room. What's waiting for me there sends me spiralling. I gasp, I scream, and tears stream down my face. *I'm sorry*, is all I can think to say. I tell him that I'm sorry. It comes out in rasping, shallow breaths between sobs. I sink to the floor and repeat the phrase again and again. *I'm sorry. I'm sorry.*

Dozens and dozens of little blue sticky notes cover the walls of the flat, roughly and jaggedly spelling out: *THIS IS YOUR FAULT*

I squeeze my eyes shut and sob into my open hands. Crumpled on the floor, I admit the truth to myself: that I can never be free of him. Even killing him wasn't enough. He's here with me. And if I turn myself in tomorrow, if I tell the police what I did, if I explain the abuse and the torment, would any of it be enough to make him go away?

I open my eyes, wipe away the stinging tears from my face, and on the floor in front of me is a single crisp blue sticky note. *YOU'RE STUCK WITH ME*, it says.

ABOUT THE AUTHOR

Willow Heath is a poet, critic, and editor based in Scotland. She is a co-founder of the literature and culture site Books and Bao, and host of the YouTube channel Willow Talks Books. Her poetry has been published in various places, both online and in print. In 2023 she narrated the audiobook for *The LGBTQ+ History Book*, and in 2024 she was shortlisted for The Poetry Lighthouse Prize.

Managing And Other Lies is her first short story collection.

booksandbao.com
youtube.com/@WillowTalksBooks
willoweditsbooks.myportfolio.com
@willowtalksbooks

Printed in Great Britain
by Amazon